DEEPEST CANYON

A STARSLINGER TALE

KRAS NEBULA

THE WHUMPY PRINTING PRESS

Cover Illustration by Hen Towers

Cover Design by Nicole Alessi

For my friends, who gave me all the feedback and support and encouragement a little guy needs to finish a book. We did it!

ALSO BY KRAS NEBULA

The Starslinger Tales
The Well

CONTENTS

— • —

Content Warnings

This story contains the following content:

- Gun violence

- Offscreen animal death

- Broken bones

- References to terminal illness and loss of a loved one

- Character death

If this book isn't for you, no worries! But if it is, we hope you enjoy this story about the post-apocalyptic wild west and all the horrors therein...

1

— · —

There was a hole in Xal's head. A clean shot, too. In through the forehead, bursting through their thick skull, cleaving through the gray matter of their brains, and puncturing right back out the other side. If it were any other spot in the body, it might be a blessing. As it was, however, it was mighty hard to find a silver lining in a bullet to the brain.

The body of Xal, all of middling height and long legs, was a foreign thing. It was still in the worn leather duster they'd been shot in, their shock of white hair against brown skin going pink with blood. Nothing more than a dressed-up slab of meat and bone, lying silent where they fell. They couldn't move a finger, couldn't feel a finger to move. They felt cold. They weren't used to feeling cold, but it weren't unfamiliar neither. Not many things are cold these days, not out in the harsh sun of the Wastes. Someone, somewhere, had told them that they ran "hot as the sun," though they could no longer remember the person's face, nor the rest of the conversation. This grasping at fog for answers only to fill their lungs with smoke was familiar too.

They floated, adrift like a sunbeam, quietly tracing where their nerves began (their damaged brain) and where they ended (somewhere else). They probed gently around the shape of a body simultaneously familiar and forgotten – the scars from a knife through their lip and bullets clustered through their chest, whose context they'd lost a long time ago; the dust baked into the creases and wrinkles of their clothes and riding leathers; the strands of long white hair that had come loose from their mooring; the callouses on their gloved hands that spoke of a lifetime of gunslinging – and tried their damnedest to remember just what it was they'd been doing, or at least what it was they were supposed to be doing. It was something important; they knew that the same way they knew where they'd been shot. The thought sat uncomfortable and weighted like a physical thing in their body until it coagulated into unpleasant certainty:

They needed to breathe.

Xal took a single, horrible, drowned-man-wheezing-corpse breath, and just like that, the world exploded into chaos.

Someone was screaming. Scratch that, *multiple* someones were screaming, and Xal couldn't rightly make out where one began or the other ended or just who was saying *what* – it all was blending into technicolor mush, and they hadn't even opened their eyes yet.

Their second breath hitched on the inhale as their nerves began lighting up, one-by-one then all at once – their neck was craned up at a wrong angle against the rugged stone wall they'd

3

slammed against upon impact, there was blood draining agonizingly slowly down their face and into their eyes and clotting in their hair, and their head –

If they thought about their head, they knew with full certainty they were going to pass out. Passing out seemed like a bad idea, given the commotion and that they still didn't know who shot them in the first place. Though they had to admit that it was tempting. Mighty tempting. Truly, undeniably tempting –

"Xal!"

Xal flinched, or at least they attempted to. Their body gave a weird shudder, like a dying fish not entirely sure what to do on land.

"Xal, can you hear me?" The stranger – someone who clearly knew them, though Xal wasn't about to pretend they could say the same – gently cradled their bloody face. Their hands were cold, small, and felt like coals against Xal's misfiring nerves. The best they could do was grunt and twitch. The stranger seemed to understand some of what plagued them, or at least assumed based off of the damage they'd already procured. Either way, the hands remained gentle, pulling the soaked strands of their hair away from their face. Someone further away snapped something, something that made the stranger tense. Like fog dissolving in the sun, Xal slowly became aware that the yelling had turned to stunned, anticipatory silence. Now it was just Xal, the stranger, and the ringing in their ears.

"Xal." The timbre of the stranger's voice had changed to something more serious. "I need you to open your eyes. Okay?" The stranger sounded young. Younger than Xal, at any rate. Scared.

It was the stranger's fear that prompted them to try more than anything else. The herculean task took just about all they had, redirecting all of their scattered focus to their eyelids and forcing the muscles to work the way they should.

The world was blurry. The light was dim. There was a face – pale, boyish, blonde hair sheared close to the stranger's head, bruise blossoming on the left cheek – hovering in front of them that lit up in sudden, hungry hope, only to immediately shift to terror as Xal's eyes rolled back into their head.

" – al!" Realistically they knew it was only a slap, and not even a particularly hard one, but the impact spider-webbed across their cheek nonetheless, and their pale eyes flew back open with a pained groan. "Xal, you can't pass out again, I'm sorry, but you can't." The stranger was babbling so quickly it would've been difficult to get a word in edgewise even if they could speak. As it was, it took all of their concentration to force the dead meat of their tongue and lips into the words "What happened?"

"Wha ... ?" was about as much as they could get out.

Silence fell, broken only by a few muffled swears and what Xal could now recognize as the other person who had spoken muttering in wonder, "Well, I'll be damned."

The stranger looked over their shoulder at the second voice only briefly before turning back to Xal. "You were shot. In the head."

Xal took another rattling breath. "Gath'r'd," they mumbled, resolving to stick to single-word answers. Maybe single-syllable, even.

The two stared for a moment, each waiting for the other to elaborate and, when it was clear an elaboration wasn't forthcoming, the stranger said with more emphasis, "Xal, you should be *dead*."

"Yup." This conversation was familiar too.

"Xal. How are you alive?!"

They shrugged, as though the answer weren't worth the effort that vocalization took. The stranger was growing increasingly horrified – personally, Xal thought they should have the opposite effect. After all, they were getting better, weren't they? But before the stranger could ask any further questions, someone else grabbed their upper arm and hauled them bodily away. They were tossed back almost nonchalantly to the others in the room, a group of blurry bandit-shaped forms Xal couldn't quite arrange into any coherent number. The person who'd tossed the stranger, a tall, thin man with slicked black hair, a thin mustache, and a suit *far* too nice and clean for the Wastes, loomed over Xal.

"Fascinating," the man said, looking Xal over like they were some kind of bug on the pavement. "No lattices, I didn't hear either of you sling a spell – not that there was time to do so. I've heard of mediums plying their trade and helping the departed move on, but I've never heard of any of them bringing someone *back*. I don't suppose you're one of those devils of the Wastes folks like to ruminate on, or perhaps one of the Wilder-Folks I'm told live among us? I've never met one before, so I can't say I know what to look for." He stopped examining Xal, his eyes roaming back up to the bullet hole in the center of their forehead. "Though, I suppose it doesn't matter. The real question is, does this happen every time you die? Or" – and he pulled out a gun, pointing it at Xal's head just a little to the left of the hole doing its best to close up – "is there a limit to how much brain matter you need to come back?"

"Alonzo, *stop*." The stranger had begun struggling against the bandits, blurry panic on their face.

The man, Alonzo, didn't take his sights off Xal and replied carelessly over his shoulder, "Sunny, darling, as curious as I am about how far this can be taken, I'm not about to waste ammunition performing this song and dance ad infinitum." He pulled the hammer back, the *click* echoing ominously in the small underground space. "I didn't have the chance to ask before, you understand."

"*Wait* – "

"Consider it a favor to your father's memory that I'm asking you now: why shouldn't I?"

"Because – " Sunny fished for words.

Xal swallowed, grumbling internally that they'd *just* been able to fully flex their hands, and now they were gonna have to start the whole process all over again.

"Because – "

They did feel bad about Sunny, though.

"Because they're an expert on 'Fore-Folk tech!"

Now, half of Xal's brains may have been splattered on the wall behind them, but they didn't think that sounded correct. Given the look of incredulity that crossed Alonzo's face, he didn't particularly believe it either.

"You're kidding me," he said. "They look more like a gun-slinger than a researcher."

"Yeah, well, I wouldn't expect you to know what someone who does fieldwork would dress like." For their part, Sunny was dressed in a well-fitting pair of working boots and an ill-fitting pair of scrapper's coveralls, just a few sizes too big with both sets having seen their share of wear, tear, and repair. "That's why I hired them, we're down in this lab for the same reason you are. Though" – and their expression managed to reach even further scorn – "I'm surprised to see *you* down here. Tired of taking the credit for the work of others? Wanted to see what all the fuss was about?"

"*For your information*, I was scrapping *long* before you ever put on the coveralls," Alonzo sniffed. "Most scrappers would understand the honor of working with me."

The room was tense, but Alonzo's attention had drifted away from Xal and there was less intent behind his hand, so Xal let their attention slip. Sunny had called it a lab, but the location they were in looked more like a cave. Felt more underground, too, like there was a nontrivial stretch of dirt between them and the open sky. If they rolled their eyes to the right, they could see the way the cavern stretched onwards and upwards, into the darkness and out of sight. They must've come in that way. If they rolled their eyes back to the center, they could see the remnants of a campsite, disturbed and trampled. A long way underground, then. Sunny was still talking, something about the make of someone's guns. They didn't see Lacey anywhere, but they also didn't see any evidence that the large, white-feathered raptor had been in the cave to begin with; likely as not they'd hid her somewhere safe on the surface after they'd dismounted.

When they rolled their eyes over to the left, they were greeted with a solid, daunting blast door, half-buried in the earth and as incongruous with the landscape as a land mine in a flower field.

Ah. A lab.

A 'Fore-Folk lab, of course, as not many present-folks and sciencey types build their labs buried deep within miles of rock. Of course, neither had the 'Fore-Folks, but the hungry earth had devised other plans when the Shattering had cracked the firmament and sent everything tits-up. It still didn't rightly explain why Xal was in one with a hole in their head, but it did begin to slot things into place.

They'd been hired by Sunny for ... reasons. Reasons that involved the lab, likely as a bodyguard or something else requiring a gun. They'd decided to rest before braving the lab itself and had been cornered by Alonzo and his cronies – six of 'em, Xal could more confidently count. Potentially only good if Alonzo's money was good, but Xal weren't in a place to challenge that loyalty, especially seeing as one of them was likely a spellslinger. Four small lights floated around the group like leaves on the wind, providing the only illumination to the scene. Alonzo and Sunny knew each other. Alonzo and Sunny were down there for the exact same reasons, and Sunny was under the impression that Xal knew what those reasons were. Or Sunny was pretending Xal did. Or Sunny was lying to keep Xal from gaining another skull piercing.

"Fine," Alonzo snapped, interrupting Sunny's bargaining and pulling Xal's attention back to him. "They can come with us. But – if either of you try anything, I won't hesitate to see how far their little reanimation trick goes."

The two bandits that had been holding Sunny with bruising force released them, and they stumbled back to Xal, placing their little body between them and Alonzo, as though his gun only had one bullet.

"I hope you got some rest," Alonzo said, holstering his gun with an unimpressed air. "We don't stop until we reach the bottom. Pick them up."

He turned away, ordering his men to focus on the blast door. Immediately Sunny was on Xal, whispering hushed apology after hushed apology while trying to find the best way to get them to their feet.

"Don't worry about me, it's not your fault," was what they meant to say, but it came out closer to "*d'ntmesn'tult.*" Fortunately, Sunny either understood what they meant or hadn't heard them as they were largely ignored. Unfortunately, Sunny had gotten themself positioned with one of Xal's limp arms around their shoulders and was preparing to lift.

Their eyes widened. They forced their traitorous tongue to form "*Wait –* "

It was too late. Sunny hefted Xal up in one solid movement, and whether it was from the sudden change in altitude or the sudden movement of a body so recently un-necrotized, Xal saw white. Their hearing narrowed to a high-pitched ringing, their joints felt bathed in acid, they were too aware of every single tooth in their mouth –

" – al? Xal, *breathe.*"

They came back to themself in agonizing spits and spurts, with every muscle screaming in unison and their head fit to explode a second time that day. It took what felt like eons to blink away the spots in their eyes, to try and reclaim some semblance of self, and even longer to remember that breathing might help. The breath they took wasn't as dramatic as the one they'd taken earlier, but it ached on the inhale and caught on the exhale. Still, Sunny held them strong and steady through the coughing fit.

"S'rry," they apologized. Sunny scoffed. "Dunno ... how much help ... I'll be."

"Don't worry," Sunny whispered back. "I'm stronger than I look."

"Ain't ... what I meant. Um ... " They trailed off, unsure how to address Sunny.

Sunny seemed to pick up on it, quickly answering, "Oh, um, Miss is fine, anything, really, that ain't Mister – Xal" – concern colored her words – "we already talked about this." The concern was rapidly shifting to horror. "Xal ... how much do you remember about where we are?"

Xal didn't have the breath to explain nor the heart to do so, so they let their eyes fall away from her face and answered her question with a stilted shrug.

"I'll ... get us ... outta here," they promised. "Guessin' ... that's why you hired me." They paused to catch their breath. "Just ... gonna need ... a minute, first."

Sunny looked as though she had something more to say, but before she could, one of the bandits passed them – a taller man, black hair cut short, the lower half of his face covered with a purple half-mask – and plopped Xal's hat back on their head, effectively covering the now-almost-closed hole. "Quiet," he snapped as he passed, though he made no move to enforce this beyond the implied threat of his rifle.

At the door, Alonzo stepped back from a sparking control panel, the interior crystal lattice beginning to shine once more. The ground rumbled, and dust fell from the ceiling as the ancient doors began to open for the first time in centuries. Sunny, Alonzo, and the bandits all watched in awe as the ancient ruins took a fresh breath of their own. Xal, though, had eyes only for Alonzo and, more importantly, what hung on Alonzo's belt, glinting in the soft illumination of the spell-lights.

"Hell," they swore. "Fucker's got my guns."

2

— · —

After the Shattering rent the world asunder and started the horrid birthing process for the world we now call our own, folks for the most part stopped building things underground. Sure, there may have been benefits to diving down deep – protection from the sun, for one – but the fear of afterquakes crushing entire settlements to paste was reason enough to stay and build on the surface. With all this in mind, it stood to reason that the only folks who would go hunting for the buried relics and tech of the 'Fore-Folks – the ones who came before – were either those who had nothing to lose or everything to gain.

Alonzo, Xal decided as the group stepped cautiously into the wide-open entry room, was probably in the latter category. The man looked as though he'd never known want in his life, or if he had, he'd forgotten what it felt like – especially if the nice, clean-pressed outfit he had on were the clothes he wore around the *Wastes*. The bandits in his employ were likely the former. Most regular folks outside of settlements were like that. It weren't entirely uncommon to see folks with such diametrically opposed lifestyles working together. Or perhaps it would be more accurate to say it weren't entirely uncommon to see folks like Dr. Alonzo Morris hiring folks like the bandit pack for any number of things: protection, muscle, using them as a force to drive honest folks off their land while simultaneously keeping their precious little hands clean.

As for Sunny ... Xal supposed they would have known where she stood vis-à-vis gaining or losing had their memory of the proceeding events not been flushed through the hole in their head. She was focused, but then Xal supposed anyone in this sort of scenario would be. They were too closely watched to even attempt to speak, which meant that any context Sunny could have given them she kept locked tight in her mouth.

Though they couldn't bring up any evidence to back up their claim, the group of bandits in Alonzo's employ seemed smaller than a group of bandits should be. Mercenaries and hired guns like themself could work easily in small or smaller groups, but the six that Alonzo had hired on as muscle read *bandit* all the way down from the scars littering their bodies to the practicality of their clothing. Other than the bandit with the purple half-mask who'd been keeping an eye on them, none of the other five gave any real care towards Xal and Sunny, letting Xal observe them in peace.

Their leader was a big bruiser type named James, who sported a wastelander tan and had his brown hair cut short. He had a scar through the bridge of his nose that had clearly been broken in one hell of a tussle, and a mean-looking rifle slung around his shoulder. Next to him, near the front of the pack, was Sylvia: tall and wiry, hair tied back in a thick braid, head on a swivel as she picked up sounds Xal couldn't even begin to hear through the ringing in their ears. Jensen, an average-sized man who clearly spent more time on the long hair pulled back into a tail than the scruffy beard on his face, similarly had his head on a swivel, but in a way that read far more like nerves than the focused way Sylvia had. In the back were Levvy and Bernard, the spellslinger and another bruiser respectively. Levvy looked a sight like James – siblings, maybe. Same skin tone, same brown hair, though she sported a single blue ribbon braided into her locks. Bernard was the biggest one yet, but seemed to hang contentedly behind Levvy and watch the rear. The bandit with the purple mask was Shui, who put as many bodies between himself and James as possible. He hung back by the prisoners, but other than the harsh reminder to stay quiet, had yet to say another word.

While Xal had no memories to base the feeling off of, something about them felt as though they weren't moving like a bandit pack *should*. Desperate, maybe. Lot of folks out in the Wastes were desperate.

Their captors, for the most part, had fallen silent the moment they stepped beyond the blast doors, guns at the ready. Levvy's spell-lights floated as high as they dared, but there was no way to illuminate both the floor in front of them and come even close to touching the monstrously high ceiling.

"Air's good," Shui commented quietly. "Might mean vents."

"Or," Alonzo interrupted, though no less quietly, "there may still be power to the filtration system, which means there may be power to other systems as well." There was a hunger to his voice that had Xal's arm hair raising and Sunny clutching them that much more tightly.

The ghost of what the entryway to the lab had once been haunted the room – the broken furniture, the decayed crystal lattices, the dead lights all hinting at a past long since left to rot. It felt unbearably empty, both achingly lonely and actively rejecting its new intruders. The small group couldn't help but feel that they shouldn't be there, that the building wanted someone *else*. But places can't think, or feel, or want the way we do, they can only groan and creak.

Perhaps that was what set everyone's spine on edge. The silence. This far underground one would expect the building to shudder with all that weight, but she held firm. Which meant any noise beyond the echoing footsteps of the group belonged to something else –

At the head of the group, just before Alonzo, James gestured sharply for the rest to halt. In the sudden silence every tiny sound was deafening: the gentle trickle of dust, the wind from further up the tunnel, the quiet scuttling of feet –

Quick as a viper, Jensen twisted and shot, his muzzle-flare bright in the darkness, and a horrible screech echoed in reply. Suddenly the room was alive with the sound of scurrying once more, but further out now and further still, squeaking in fear as they retreated. The critter that had been hit continued to make its horrible, screeching, wounded animal cries all the way up until James stalked over and shot it again.

"Burrowers," he said, curling his lip.

Given the raptors and tri-horns and spikebacks of the surface world, burrowers could hardly be considered large. At a little under hip-height, though, they weren't exactly small, closer to a good-sized dog than anything. Between the feathers, the two legs, and the two short arms hosting their digging claws, they weren't unlike raptors. Save, of course, for the lack of meat in their diet and their propensity to scurry around and dig tunnels into the earth instead of run out under the sun. Most of the time they kept to their tunnels and to themselves, and were generally considered not much beyond a nuisance.

"Ah, yes, a worthy adversary and one well worth waking up anything else still around," Alonzo snapped scathingly. Jensen had the good sense to look sheepish, though no less nervous.

"Come on, Doc, no need for that," James drawled before looking over at one of his own. "Sylvia?"

Sylvia had taken her station crouched by one of the disintegrated chairs. "Just more burrowers, Boss," she called. "Don't seem like they're nesting here, but based off the droppings and tracks, I'd wager there's a host of burrower's tunnels in these walls. This place is just a juncture, a, uh, train station, if you will," she elaborated, seemingly for Alonzo's benefit. The doctor did not look particularly appreciative of this gesture.

"What she's saying," James stepped in once more, "is that if they feel safe enough to move about in the open like this, then ain't nothin' eating them down here. Nothin' else has been living here since the 'Fore-Folks were. Ease up a little."

Doctor Alonzo Morris did not, in fact, ease up, and instead only prickled further at the insinuation that he should.

"Just because these ruins are derelict," he bit out, "does not mean they are dead."

Underneath Xal's arm, Sunny flinched – an almost mechanical movement and one she clearly had tried to stop. At Alonzo's words the rest of the bandits shifted uneasily; Jensen had his head on a swivel, twitching at any sudden movement or noise; Sylvia had made herself smaller, looking quizzically around and focusing on the layout of the room and the patches of particularly deep darkness; Levvy had stepped closer to Bernard, who'd made himself a larger target; James kept his head high and the grip on his gun tight; Shui inched ever closer to his prisoners, just within grabbing range. Whether that was to pull them into or out of danger, Xal couldn't rightly tell.

"Well," Alonzo spoke, causing the entire group to jump, "if something were to attack us, I assume it either would have done so, or it already has us in its sights. Let us move forwards, hopefully having learned something from this."

Their steps echoed in the empty room, maybe not as deafening as the gunshots had been but loud enough to set the group on edge. Every now and then Jensen would startle-flinch and point his gun at shadows or more burrowers, sending them skittering away to safety.

"Weak link," Xal murmured out of the corner of their mouth. Sunny hummed a question back at them. "Jumpy one," Xal elaborated. "Could be easy to distract."

"Maybe," Sunny muttered back just as quietly. "But what 'bout the others? 'Sides, you can hardly move."

"I'm" – Xal paused to tamp down on a groan as Sunny maneuvered them around a pile of debris – "workin' on it."

Problem was, Sunny wasn't wrong. The forces piecing Xal's brain back together had apparently decided that sensory input was more important than motor control, leaving them uncomfortably awake and alert as their limp body was dragged across the room. They felt every single nauseating bump and sway but could do absolutely nothing about it but brace and pray. Talk of escape aside, a nontrivial part of Xal was already wishing for a break. "Listen – " they started.

"Quiet," Shui interrupted sharply. Xal half-expected a shove to accompany his words, but Shui kept his hands carefully on his rifle. He clearly knew where his priorities lay, and they were not in shoving around prisoners who could barely walk. That alone had Xal on edge. Jensen may have been the weak link, but they would be hard-pressed to find an opening with Shui watching them like a hawk.

At the other side of the room, past the decayed remains of some kind of front desk, there were two sets of doors. The first set were the same sort of imposing, solid blast doors that had led into the ruins. The second were smaller, set into the wall a story above and connected to the ground by a set of questionable stairs. With neither discussion nor hesitation Alonzo led the group up the stairs, wincing with every creak and groan of the ancient metal.

Xal clung tightly to Sunny as best they could as they ascended, step by step, each one an effort. Sunny bore them wordlessly, save for a few quiet apologies when their brown face turned white and their sweat glistened in the spell-lights.

"Sunny, be a dear and hurry it up, would you? I need your hands in here," Alonzo called from somewhere beyond the doors.

"Might've been faster," Sunny grunted, heaving Xal's body up another step, "if you hadn't shot one of us in the *head.*"

Despite the nauseating agony still beating from their brain, Xal huffed a breathless laugh. "Think ... if we take too long ... " they said between breaths, "he'll shoot me again?"

"Don't tempt me."

Xal began a retort, but before they could fire it off, Sunny's grip on them tightened like a vise. Not something to joke about, then.

They had barely a moment to catch their breath at the top of the stairs before James grabbed Sunny by the arm and hauled her into the room, leaving Xal to tumble bonelessly to the floor.

"Hey – !" She attempted to lunge towards Xal, but James's grip was locked tight around her arm.

Alonzo rolled his eyes. "They survived a bullet to the head, I'm sure they're fine." Xal, for their part, gave a wheezing groan from the floor but otherwise made no move to get up. "You, however, I need over here." He gestured to the larger part of what could now be recognized as, likely, some kind of security room. A jumble of identical screens sat bolted to the wall, an input terminal underneath; the entire thing was dark and dead as could be, not even leaving an errant spark of life. "I would like to have an idea of the layout of this place before we go any deeper. Get it working."

There was a danger to Sunny's glare, but it just as quickly fizzled out into something more resentful but resigned as Shui took his place once more over Xal. "Fine," she spat, yanking her arm out of James's hold and disappearing into the workings of the machine, "but I'll need your spellslinger."

There are very few folks these days who can work the tech of the old world, who can even begin to wrap their mind around the complicated crystal lattices and magical frequencies the 'Fore-Folks used before they blew themselves into the firmament, but of that small group of folks, Scrappers make up a solid percent. Sunny quickly grew silent as her deft hands wove their way into the wires and lattices, muttering to herself as she puzzled her way around the ancient technology and occasionally asking Levvy for a whistled note.

Xal lost time. They didn't have the mobility to maneuver themself out of the heap they'd landed in, and it didn't seem like anyone else was about to help them out of it, so they drifted. They let sound filter in and out of their ears and the now mostly-closed hole in their head; Sunny's tinkering, Alonzo's cruel remarks, dust falling from the ceiling, the skittering of burrower claws, and, further, something else.

They must've lost more time than they thought, as when next they opened their eyes – eyes they didn't remember closing, granted – Shui had just finished propping them upright against the wall of the security room. "Y'all hear that...?" they rasped. The room immediately fell still.

"Hear what?" Alonzo asked after a beat. The bandits shifted, Jensen in particular gripping his gun a little more tightly.

Xal took a breath, then another. "There's somethin' out there."

Every occupant strained their senses to try and hear what it was Xal had picked up on. Dust. The scrabbling of tiny claws. The tapping of something metallic against the stone cavern –

Just as quickly as it had sounded, the noise stopped as though someone, or something, had silenced it.

"I – I don't like this," Jensen stammered.

James grunted before turning back to where Sunny was still half-inside the terminal. "How much longer?"

"Almost got it – " came the strained reply.

"Alright. Jensen, take the door. 'S probably nothin', but I ain't taking chances."

Jensen didn't look happy at the posting, but he did seem to prefer it over waiting to be ambushed. The silence that fell afterwards was tense, each person straining their senses just in case, none of them daring to make small talk on the off chance something else was listening.

"Got it!" The entire room started – or, in Xal's case, made an involuntary twitch – as the monitors lit up and Sunny pushed herself back out from the terminal. As the monitors lit up one by one, the emergency lights gave their best flicker, casting a dim light around the room.

"Well, I'll be," James muttered in wonder. "Shit down here's usually dead for good."

"No, most folks just don't know how to turn it back on." There was a hint of pride in Sunny's voice, even as she shook her hands out. "'Fore-Folks had a greater handle on their tech than the rest of y'all, these babies can hold a charge indefinitely so long as the lattice ain't broke and you can get a spark – hey!"

At a look from Alonzo, Sylvia had grabbed Sunny and shoved her next to Xal. "Yes, yes, very interesting, I'm sure," Alonzo said without looking back and began flicking through the readouts on the monitors. Images and words too far away to read flashed by, though Xal was certain some of that had to do with how their vision hadn't fully cleared.

"How're you doing?" Sunny asked quietly, taking advantage of Alonzo's focus on the machine.

"Been better," they grunted.

"Xal."

"Right, right." As best they could, Xal widened their hands, stretching out their fingers before curling them into weak fists. It wasn't much, but it was progress. They moved their arms slowly – not for any kind of notion of stealth, but because that was the one speed they had at the moment – and placed their palms flat on the concrete floor and *pushed*. They made it barely an inch before their arms gave out, and they collapsed back against the wall with an exhausted breath.

"Might be a bit yet," they grumbled after taking a moment to catch their breath.

"That's not what I'm asking," Sunny admonished quietly.

"Head hurts. Can't shoot. Not sure what else you want." Their words were short, curt, but they got the point across, and Sunny sat back with a huff.

"*Xal.*" At this Xal finally looked up and met Sunny's eyes. They might not've remembered her or how circumstance had thrown them together, but they could recognize the kind of emotional cocktail of someone worried out of their wits for someone who couldn't quite understand *why* in her face. "You *died.*"

"Didn't stick ... " They trailed off into silence as Sunny's frown deepened.

"How much do you remember?" Sunny asked, lowering her voice further.

"My name. Lacey. How to ride." The words felt familiar, like they'd answered the question a million times before. Their eyes moved away from Sunny to the two elegant pistols, mother-of-pearl, golden inlay, that had been shoved into Alonzo's belt. *Xal's* pistols. "How to shoot." They turned back to Sunny. "But ... as for why we're here, ain't got much to say. Mind filling me in?"

Sunny sat back and dragged a tiny, exhausted hand across her face. When she opened her eyes, they'd hardened. "Right," she whispered. "Keep that to yourself." So much for context.

Xal frowned. "Sunny?" they said, with all the gravity they could muster. "I'm gonna get you out of this." That was likely their job, far as they could guess.

Sunny, however, didn't seem to agree. Her expression shifted into something darker still, her hands clenching into solid fists.

"Sunny!" Alonzo barked from the monitors. "Get over here."

Sunny bit down on whatever she'd been about to say and moved out of Xal's reach.

"Most of the cameras are either non-functional or in rooms too dark to get a look at, but we've found a map." Alonzo carelessly tossed a miniature lattice to her. It was formed of a single circle, with pink crystals inlaid equidistant from one another and all pointing towards the center, which held another crystal that had been cut into a perfect cube. The entire thing buzzed in her hand with untapped energy. Sunny's eyes widened, turning the delicate lattice in the dim light.

"Where did you ... ?" she wondered.

"Transfer the map to the lattice," Alonzo interrupted. "I have no doubt certain sections have been affected by time, and I would rather not stumble around such sections blindly." When Sunny hesitated, he quirked an eyebrow. "I know you know how to do this. Your father used to rave about your skill with 'Fore-Folk lattices."

Xal hadn't thought Sunny's glare could reach new depths, but there was a shift in her stance. A stiffness, a danger.

Alonzo sighed, pulled out one of Xal's guns, and aimed it at them. They tensed, grasping for any possible way they could avoid the shot and coming up empty. "*Now*, Miss Quill."

The panic left Sunny's eyes only to be replaced with cold resignation, and she stepped back to the console.

"Pity," Alonzo purred, admiring Xal's gun. "I would have loved to see what these do. Plasmashot, it looks like, but not a make or model I recognize. Where did you get these?"

"They're *mine*," Xal growled.

Alonzo frowned. "Not anymore, and not what I asked. Were they custom? They must be, from the seal on the handle. Who is your gunsmith? Unless you found them somewhere, which, if you're half the 'expert' Sunny says, I could almost believe."

"*Bite me.*" Xal was growing increasingly tired of their captor. Unfortunately it seemed the opinion went both ways as, with a sharp look from Alonzo, James's boot collided with Xal's face, snapping their head to the side and making them see nothing but stars. When they pulled themself back, blood sharp against their numb tongue, Sunny was shouting again.

" – re harmless! You don't have to do this, I'm doing what you asked!"

"They bounced back from a bullet to the head, I can't imagine a boot to the face will do much worse." Alonzo wasn't wrong, but Xal couldn't help but feel apprehensive of the fact that he was beginning to collect data on the subject. The shouting continued as Xal did their damnedest to pull their eyelids back open, interrupted only by Shui's occasional interjection, and amongst it all they could hear the echoing metallic tapping growing closer –

Xal pried their eyes open just as the building lights plunged into darkness, only to be replaced a moment later with flashing red lights. Garbled messages that may have once been words echoed from speakers long since decayed, the voice who had recorded them long since dead.

"What did you do?!" screamed Jensen from his place at the door, aiming his rifle wildly into the room. "*What did you do*?!"

"Me?! I didn't do anything!" Sunny protested, the miniature lattice held tightly in her hands.

"Then – "

Whatever Jensen had been about to say was lost. From beyond and above the doorway, two metallic, reticulated arms stretched forward, ending in wicked, articulated claw-tipped hands. The most Jensen ever saw of his death were the red lights reflecting off of black metal in his periphery before the claws dug into his neck and shoulder and *pulled*, yanking his flailing body out and upwards towards the ceiling, screaming all the way.

For a moment no one moved, stunned to silence in the cacophony of Jensen's final gargled cries and the garbled message over the ancient intercoms.

James moved first, swearing loudly and bolting for the doorway, finger already on the trigger –

"*Stop*!" Alonzo yelled. "He's already dead. I hired you to protect *me*."

James turned on him, looming with his full impressive height. "*You don't know that*!"

Shui shook his head. "It's carrying him upwards, even if we shot it down, he wouldn't be able to survive a fall like that – " Right on cue, Jensen's cries were cut off horribly quick, and seconds later there was the unmistakable wet *thump* of a body hitting the floor somewhere in the greater chamber.

"We can't stay here!" Sylvia hissed.

"And I suppose going outside where *it* is waiting is the more intelligent option, rather than where it only has one avenue to attack us?" Alonzo sneered. "What am I saying, I don't pay you dogs to *think*."

At the corner of the room, much forgotten, Sunny had quietly moved back to Xal and slipped their arm over her bony shoulder. "When I say 'go,' jump with whatever you got."

Xal didn't think they had much to give, but they curled their fingers in her coveralls with one hand, braced against the ground with their other, and bent and tensed their legs as best they could.

"Be *very* careful about the next thing you say," James growled.

"Or you'll what? Shoot me? Lose out on your payment?" There was a dangerous glint in Alonzo's eye. "Already down a pack member with nothing to show for it. If you back out now, you'll wind up worse than you started with – "

"*Go.*"

Xal did their absolute best to help, but they didn't need to hold as much of their weight as they thought they'd have to as Sunny sprang to the door with shocking speed.

"Stop her!" Alonzo screeched.

She descended the steps two at a time, jarring Xal with every step. Bernard sprang first out of the doorway and fired a shot that cracked the stairs under Sunny's feet, sending them both tumbling to the ground in a heap.

"Not another step!" he called. "Not if you want another hole in the – " His voice broke off into a scream as the shadow that had been advancing down the wall above him snapped out, horrible arms reaching down to grab him by the face and shoulders and bodily fling him from the landing, tearing bloody chunks from his body as he went ragdolling through the air to *slam* through one of the ancient desks.

"*Bernard!*" Levvy screamed from inside.

"*Up up up –* " Sunny mumbled frantically, getting her feet under her and hauling Xal upright.

"Sunny – " Xal sucked in a breath as the room tilted alarmingly. "Sunny, I'm dead weight, you gotta *go.*"

"No." Sunny slung Xal's arm back over her shoulder.

"*Sunny –* " But as she took a step, Xal's busted brain realized something. "Sunny, the exit ain't that way."

"*I know,*" Sunny growled as she dragged them to the heavy blast door that led deeper into the laboratory.

With a furious yell, James flung himself onto the landing and began unloading bullet after bullet into the creature clinging to the wall – only for the bullets to ricochet harmlessly off the metal carapace. In the light of the gunfire, pieces of the creature could be made out: the heavy black metal plating, the humanoid body structure tilted sideways with heavy claws and flexible joints, the unflinching faceplate staring down the barrel of James's gun.

"*Move,*" Alonzo ordered before raising Xal's pilfered pistol. With a single shot, the cavern was bathed in blinding light, the plasma breaking across the faceplate like a wave. The creature reared back, sparks flying and illuminating the metal joints, hissing and clawing its way back up into the darkness.

"Grab her, you idiots! *She's got the map!*" Alonzo shouted as he shot wildly with Xal's gun. The cavernous space lit up with each shot like a crack of lightning, blindingly bright then plunged back into darkness. Each shot illuminated a different scene – Sunny dropping Xal to the ground to fiddle with the door; James and Sylvia sprinting after them; Levvy searching frantically around the cavern with her spell-lights while Shui kept his rifle at the ready; the mechanical creature clinging to the side of the cavern, watching.

In a flash, James had reached Sunny, cracking the back of his hand across her face and sending her sprawling to the floor. The control panel she'd been tinkering with sparked and fizzed, and the blast door began opening and closing, opening and closing.

"Just come with us, nice and – " Sylvia ended her sentence with a *whoop* as Xal snagged her ankle from the floor and gave a mighty *tug*, sending her toppling to the ground. Before they could make good on their move, however, Sylvia scrambled out of reach, drawing her gun and aiming it directly at Xal.

"Not another move, neither of you," she snapped, "or it's bullet number two."

"Alright," James said, hauling Sunny upright by the arm. "Let's get a move on while we still can." He took a breath then, in the brief second that the door was open, leapt through to the other side, pulling Sunny along with him. "You next, Doc."

Alonzo stumbled over Xal's body, eyes wide and limbs jittery, before returning to the door and jumping through as quick as he could.

In the dark, something moved.

"Shui."

Shui backed in slowly, eyes scanning the darkness, before ducking through.

"Levvy."

Levvy's hand was glued to her mouth, and with a sharp whistle, her four lights followed her through the door, leaving the room solely lit by the emergency lights.

"Sylvia."

Sylvia kept her gun trained on Xal until the last possible second as she followed suit.

"Wait, what about Xal?" Sunny protested, struggling against the iron grip on her arm. Xal, for their part, looked at the rapidly opening and closing metal of the blast door, then down at their tangle of legs. There was no way they would be able to get themself through on their own.

With one person left outside the safety of the blast doors, the metal creature dropped to the floor, running on all fours at a gallop.

"Aw hell – " Xal summoned what strength they had and *dragged* themself as best as they could backwards – but nowhere near fast enough. Their legs refused to push under them, to carry them to safety, but they crawled with all they had in their arms until their back hit the chomping maw of the blast door.

"It's coming – "

"So shoot it!"

Alonzo fired Xal's gun once more, the heat and light of the solar pulse burning the ends of their hair as it blew past, only to miss wildly. Again the gun fired and *again* the bolt missed, and despite the situation Xal couldn't stop the bloom of rage in their stomach at the waste.

"*Levvy, take it down!*"

"But my lights – "

"Do it!"

Levvy released four sharp notes, and as the spell-lights winked out of existence, the air around the creature pulsed violently, vibrating its joints and causing it to shudder and shake and grind against itself – but the creature kept coming, no matter how the ancient machinery around them vibrated with Levvy's frequencies.

"For fuck's sake – " Shui's muttered swearing was the only warning Xal got before they were grabbed by the scruff of their duster and *hauled* through the door. They blinked the spots from their eyes just in time to witness Shui snatch the gun from Alonzo with his free hand and blast the creature right in the face. A metallic screech echoed through the halls from the creature, causing Sunny to slap her hands over her ears.

As the door slammed shut once more, Shui grabbed the ends and held them closed on his own steam. "James! Give me a hand!"

With Shui on one side and James on the other, Sylvia grabbed Xal's gun from Shui and melted the door shut.

Not a moment too soon. The blast door *buckled* as the creature flung itself at it, the metal bending and warping under its onslaught. Metal upon metal shrieked as it shifted to using its horrible claws.

BOM

BOM

BOM

... And then silence, save for the distorted alarm echoing throughout the facility.

3

— · —

For a moment no one moved – they all stood still in the hall, staring at the welded blast door and breathing heavily in the dim, red light.

"What in every hell – " James murmured before he was cut off by Sylvia delivering a thunderous kick to Xal's torso.

"Snag me by the ankle, huh?" she snarled, kicking them again. "Thought you could scrabble off and get the best of me, huh?" Another kick. "Should've just left you out there to get torn apart by that metal devil!" Kick, kick, kick. Had they the chance to catch their breath, Xal would've snagged her and toppled her a second time. As it were, they were finding it mighty hard to do much of anything beyond cough and wheeze on the dusty floor.

"*Stop it!*" Sunny rushed forward. "They're – "

She pulled up short, staring down the barrel of James's rifle. "We know how they're doing. We made 'em like that," James drawled, low and dangerous. "And the next time you two get it in your heads to run, I'm shooting both of you, 'expert knowledge' be damned. Are we clear?"

Sunny watched as Sylvia delivered one final blow, leaving Xal wheezing on their back, before leveling her gaze back at James. "Crystal," she said, not quite hiding the tremble in her voice.

James held her gaze for a moment longer before nodding at Shui to stand over Xal. "Good. Levvy, lights." A short set of whistles and Levvy's spell-lights had returned. Folks breathed slightly more easily, even if they didn't notice. "Now, seems to me you two have lost close quarters privileges. Shui, keep the gunslinger with you in the back; Sunny here gets to go with us in the front." He paused, waiting to be interrupted or reprimanded for taking charge, but no words ever came. He turned back to Alonzo, who was still standing stock-still, staring at the door. " ... Doc?"

"Did you see how it moved?" he murmured, the glow from the gun in his hand casting flickering shadows on the wall as his hand trembled. "The articulation, the construction – it hardly *flinched* at the bullets ... What a marvel."

"*Doc*!" James repeated himself, sharper this time. At this Alonzo started, almost dropping Xal's gun before remembering where exactly he was and, more importantly, who he was with. He straightened himself out, holstered Xal's gun, and coughed awkwardly.

"Yes, yes, what is it?" he snapped.

"What the hell was that thing?" Levvy asked quietly.

37

"A construct, of course," Alonzo said, as though it were the most obvious thing in the universe, which, within certain contexts and preconceived notions, it was. Most folks out in the Wastes and beyond had at least heard about constructs: the fallen corpses of the old world, rusted shut with their lattices crumbled to dust. Rare up on the surface, but common enough for scrappers and the like. No one was quite sure what they were made of, or how the 'Fore-Folks had gotten them to move as they supposed they must have, but they were built for a variety of purposes from the smallest, most delicate tasks to the largest hauling ventures. Farming, guarding, medical ... well, most of that was all speculation from where they were found and what they looked like, and most of them had been found in pieces, anyways.

"No, no, that can't be right," Sylvia said, shaking her head.

"And why not?"

"Because it *moved*." Sylvia threw an arm out towards the crumpled blast door. "No one's ever seen one *move* before, they're all supposed to be *dead*, how the *hell* is it moving?!"

"I ... I'm not sure," Alonzo admitted. "According to most records, what the 'Fore-Folks had built was destroyed in the Shattering; by all rights it *shouldn't* be, but if I could get my hands on it ... "

Sunny shifted nervously.

"Alright," James sighed. "Do you at least know what kind it is?"

"Silencer Mk. 5." Everyone's heads snapped to the floor where Xal had spoken. "Or somethin' similar. I don't think the Mk. 5's were quite that big, they were supposed to be small enough to get into places, take folks out all quiet-like. Didn't think they ever made it to Mk. 6, though."

" ... How the *hell* do you know this?" Alonzo asked, clearly more befuddled than sore that someone knew more than him.

Xal had no right clue any more than he did, but they weren't about to tell him that. "Didn't Sunny say I was an expert?"

Sunny very quickly tooled her expression away from surprise, as though she'd known the whole time. "Told you."

"Great. We've got an ancient assassin construct after us," James sighed. "Frankly that don't change too much. What's our next move, Doc?"

With the conversation shifting away from the marvel hunting them through the building, all wonder left Alonzo. He snagged Sunny by the arm and wrenched the map away from her. Once again the delicate crystal lattice sparked to life, displaying a series of flickering maps and floor layouts. Alonzo flicked through them in silence before pointing a finger.

"We are here," he said, causing the others to peer over his shoulder – all, save for Xal and Sunny. The two made eye contact. Sunny made a concerned face. "This building goes down several floors, and I find it doubtful we'll get too much up here beyond office space and administrative areas."

"I take it you've done something like this before?" Shui asked carefully. From the ground, quite unnoticed, Xal gave a shaky thumbs-up.

"Of course," Alonzo sniffed. Sunny's face shifted from concern to suspicion. "What do you take me for, an amateur?"

Shui didn't respond immediately to that, but though his expression was difficult to read under the half-mask, he set his shoulders a bit more defensively. Under him Xal paused, thought, then delivered a second thumbs-up. Sunny relaxed slightly.

"We won't be getting out the same way," Shui tried again. "Should probably keep on the lookout for another exit." Xal's eyes flicked up towards Shui, then Sylvia, James, Levvy, and finally Alonzo before silently holding up a hand with all five fingers splayed.

"Of course," Alonzo snapped, flicking through with increasing speed. Sunny gave a hint of a nod before frowning and mimicking a gun with her hand. Her frown turned into a look of incredulity as Xal waved dismissively. She shifted her hand to her mouth, mimicking a whistle. When Xal was equally as dismissive, she rolled her eyes in disbelief. She looked as though she were about to mime something else when Alonzo turned back towards Sunny.

"You," he snapped. "This lab is the sister lab to the one Dr. Quill excavated, yes?"

Sunny stared. "How do ... how do you know that? How did you even know where to find this place?"

To his credit, Alonzo's expression slipped. "Dr. Quill sent me a letter detailing how to get here," he said quietly. "I was supposed to do this with him."

Sunny's mouth hung open. "He – he would *never*. You two hated each other."

"He didn't run it by you first?" Alonzo tutted. "A pity. Of course, I'd originally refused but then, well." There was a beat before he asked, "How did it happen?"

It took Sunny a few tries to get the words out. They were still too heavy for her small mouth, even in a place like this. "A heart attack," she said, finally. "Three weeks ago."

To his credit, a hint of confused grief made its way into Alonzo's expression. "I ... can't say I'm overjoyed to hear that. I had lunch with him just before. A heart attack of all things ... " He trailed off before returning to the topic at hand. "Still, he must have told you about the other lab, yes?"

"That ... that was before my time." Sunny couldn't meet his eyes, even as he pressed further into her space.

"But not by much, not by much at all." He towered over her, and she shrank back. "Don't lie to me, Sunny Quill."

She swallowed, took a breath. "Experimental 'Fore-Folk con-structs," she said finally. "They were very early, hardly anything completed. It was likely they'd gotten to work just before the Shattering, so they'd never managed to get particularly far with

41

any of them – not like the one outside. Weren't nothing of use beyond the historical, most were broken beyond repair."

"But there *were* some things of value, yes?"

Sunny seemed to glean what the Doctor was getting at, and for a moment that steel slipped back into her spine. Her eyes flicked back to Xal, however, and when she turned back to Alonzo it was with less resolve. " ... The basement levels," she said, looking away. "That's where they'll be keeping the bigger projects."

"Good girl." Alonzo ruffled her short hair and Sunny bristled.

"There's no guarantee the lower levels even survived the Shattering," she said, raising her voice. "Or if there's even still a way down!"

"We also don't know what else is awake down here." The attention in the room shifted as Shui spoke up. "It's a safe bet this is also some kinda construct lab, if that thing that attacked us is any indication." He shook his head. "We need to find a new way out and take it. We're already down two and – "

In two strides James had crossed the distance and grabbed a strangling hold on the back of Shui's neck, forcing his head down. "Tryin' to give orders again, Shui? Thinkin' of turning your back again?" The pressure increased. "Because that worked out so well for you last time, didn't it?" Shui stayed silent, his eyes trained on the floor. "If you weren't so good a shot, I would've tossed you to the Wastes after the last stunt you pulled." Levvy looked away, clearly uncomfortable with the confrontation; in stark contrast, Sylvia looked on in glee. When it was clear Shui had no intention of speaking up, James pulled back, clapping him on the shoulder. "Just think of the payout when this is over."

Xal and Sunny shared a look, and for once there was no need for exaggerated pantomiming. They both could tell what the other was thinking: this was something they could use.

"James, he's got a point," Levvy spoke up quietly. "We don't know what else is down here."

In sharp contrast to how he'd spoken to Shui, the way James looked at Levvy was downright saccharine. "It'll be fine, Levs. We'll take it slow, keep an eye out. Like I said, think of the payout." Levvy clearly was still worried, but she nodded along anyway.

Alonzo sniffed. "If you're quite done, I suggest we get moving ... "

BOM

He trailed off into startled silence as noises echoed through the halls. It was hard to tell which direction they came from, but everyone's eyes snapped to a different angle, the arguments largely forgotten. The seconds ticked by agonizingly slowly before the rumbling stopped, somewhere off in the larger labyrinth of the dilapidated building.

The coast was clear, at least for that moment. James nodded to Alonzo. "Right. Let's get a move on."

Now, a scrapper's life ain't an easy one, and that is namely due to the location in which a scrapper scraps. Sure, folks might argue of the dangers those that travel the Wastes from settlement to settlement have to deal with, but frankly all the ways those folks die – bandits, heat exhaustion, falling into a canyon when they weren't lookin' – are right natural. No one knew precisely what killed the 'Fore-Folks, but from the environments they left behind, "natural" didn't come even close to describing their fate. The ruins in which scrappers scrapped were, more often than not, museums of the unnatural: spellwork common folks couldn't even begin to comprehend, constructs and machines and lattices that made the soul ache just to look at, experiments left behind where the only understanding of what they'd been trying to accomplish was from horrific implications. Every scrapper worth their salt knew the dangers of touching something unknown in a 'Fore-Folk ruin, and every scrapper had at least one story about a friend who was never quite the same after they'd done just that. It's common knowledge, after all, that the 'Fore-Folks had caused the Shattering, and thus had been the ones to blow themselves to smithereens alongside half the world.

And if they could do that, who knew what else they had gotten up to?

It was with this thought in mind that the group moved slowly down the hall, everyone on high alert despite the seemingly benign office spaces they passed. Some doors remained open, others barred shut, and still others had cracked and fallen when the world had ended. In this day and age there generally weren't skeletons to find – bones crushed or eaten or absorbed or in some other way succumbed to entropy – but the resulting emptiness of the labs, decaying desks and chairs and other such things, created the illusion that those who'd once spent their lives working there just ... got up and left one day.

"Shouldn't we be checking these rooms?" Sylvia asked from her spot in the middle of the group.

"If you want to lug equipment around for the rest of the excavation, be my guest," Alonzo sneered, "but I doubt you'll find anything of use up here. Why bother with the small things when a treasure trove awaits us?"

If Sylvia had anything more to say, she was distracted by the hall ending in a T, the doors of the building elevator sitting rusted shut. James sighed. "Shui, help me get this open."

"Are you sure the elevator is the smartest option?" Sunny asked as the two men began struggling with the door.

"According to the map, there are thirty floors. I don't know about you, but I, for one, have no interest in climbing that many steps if I do not absolutely have to." Alonzo pulled the map back up, studying the various floors as though to confirm his own statement.

With a grunt and the screech of rusted metal, the elevator doors were opened, revealing a pitch-black shaft, the echoes traveling for much longer than anyone felt comfortable with.

"Sunny, if you will," Alonzo ordered.

"Yeah, yeah," Sunny grumbled as she elbowed her way to the ancient control panel and pried it open with some effort. Immediately the dim red emergency lights were overpowered by a sharp flash of fuchsia as the crystal lattice sparked violently before crumbling to dust with a horrid purple fizzle. Sunny coughed, waving the smoke away.

"Don't suppose you can lower us down easy-like?" James asked, turning to Levvy.

Levvy chewed on her lip, looking down into the abyss before shaking her head. "Not that far. That spell only lasts as long as I can hold the note, but I can't do that for thirty floors, not on your life."

Alonzo huffed, closing the map and shoving it in his pocket. "I guess we shall have to settle for the stairs after all. This – "

BOM

Alonzo started, then coughed awkwardly. " – Um, this way."

It was with a slightly quicker pace that the group pressed onwards, everyone keeping a watchful eye out. Every darkened room was a space to be hidden in, every shadow a creature waiting to strike. Occasionally more noises would echo through the building, but it was difficult to say just where they were echoing *from*, and how whatever made them seemed to be getting there. There was no question that the construct knew the building better; it was just a matter of time before it caught up with them. Without speaking, the various members of the group came to the same conclusion on their own, and all clumped a little closer together.

"The stairs should be right around this – " Alonzo's words left him in a gasp as he turned the corner and stepped nearly over the edge of a massive pit that swallowed the hallway. Had it not been for James's hand snagging the back of his well-pressed shirt and dragging him back, that would have been the end of Doctor Alonzo Morris. On the other side of the pit where the stairwell should have been was nothing more than rubble and debris and further cracks in the masonry. Alonzo huffed a sigh, attempting to cover his panic at nearly falling to his death, and scrubbed a hand through his hair that was no longer quite so in place as it had been only moments before. "Well, I suppose we'll just have to find a new route." He pulled up the map and began frantically scanning through it, muttering to himself.

James peered over the side of the pit. "Lights," he ordered, and with a sharp whistle, the spell-lights moved from where they'd encircled the group and floated down the pit like a strand of glowing pearls. The light only reached so far, but the pit reached fairly deep. James clicked his tongue against his teeth. "That's what, fifteen? Twenty stories?" He looked back at Levvy, who immediately began shaking her head.

"No, that's still too far, there's no way I can hold a note that long," she protested.

James slung an arm around her shoulder. "You won't have to, just long enough to get down a few stories so you can catch your breath, y'know. Do it in spurts instead of all at once. What do you think, Doc? A sight faster than trying to find a new route that might not exist."

"And how exactly are we supposed to get back up?" Sunny muttered under her breath. She was ignored by everyone save Shui, who sent a sympathetic glance back.

"Surely you don't expect me to just *jump* that, do you?" Alonzo asked, peering down into the darkness.

"Naw, we can make it." James slung his rifle across his back and gave Levvy a wink. "You won't let me fall, right?" Levvy looked unsure but shook her head nonetheless. Without further comment, James took a running start and leaped into the pit. There was a fraction of a second before Levvy got her hand to her mouth and whistled out a sustained note that vibrated out from her spine and through her hand and caused the long-broken lattices still scattered in the various offices to hum with confused echoes. James's downward descent slowed like he'd fallen into water, still moving forward with his momentum, but when he reached the other side about three floors down, he hit the ground as though he'd only leaped off a six foot wall.

"What did I say?" He pulled himself to his feet and gave a mock salute. "Ain't nothin' to it, and a sight faster than going the long way." Levvy shook her hand out and caught her breath. "I figure if we station folks every few floors, we can catch them as they come down, ferry 'em easy-like." When Alonzo still looked unsure, he continued, "It's this or the elevator shaft, Doc. I dunno about you, but I'd rather do this than try to rappel down for thirty stories."

"Fine," Alonzo sniffed, "but I'm not going next."

Sylvia went next, followed by Shui, the two of them situating themselves on either side of the pit with roughly three floors between them. Those left on the top floor waited anxiously, knowing that the longer they took, the closer the construct got. As such, when it came his time to jump, for all his loud hesitation earlier, Alonzo jumped with perhaps a bit *too* much eagerness, spindly limbs windmilling as he crossed the gap one, two, three times over. Once he'd landed safely next to Shui, Levvy called for a break, breathing deep to try and get her wind back.

"Think you can do it?" Sunny asked Xal quietly. They'd been shoved at her when the others had gone down; apparently the bandits were confident in their lack of places to escape to, or confident in Levvy's ability to stop them. Xal's own confidence in their ability to make it to the bottom wasn't quite so firm, but they weren't about to say that out loud.

"Don't think I got much choice – " They paused, mid-sentence, listening. Sunny froze, listening as well –

BOM

Closer, now, uncomfortably close. Alonzo's voice echoed up from below, "Alright, that's enough of a break. Move along, now."

Levvy took another deep breath and let it out slowly before looking between Sunny and Xal. "Which one's next?"

"Xal," Sunny said quickly, hauling them over to the edge. Levvy took another breath –

BOM

– only for it to shudder out uncertainly. "Okay. On three, push them over the side with as much force as you've got. One, two, *three* – "

Sunny shoved Xal over the side with all her might, and for a second they were falling – before Levvy's whistle filled the air and caught them, making them light and buoyant like a stick sinking gently in a pond. For the first time in about an hour, Xal felt relatively painless with the spell lifting all their weight off their bruised and battered nervous system. They drifted slower than the others, though; not as much momentum. Levvy was forced to hold the note longer than she had for the others.

BOM

It was getting closer.

BOM

Closer. Xal was almost halfway across the gap. James reached out impatiently towards them.

CLANG

One of the vent covers went flying across the hallway, bouncing off the far wall and clattering to the ground. From the vent emerged the sleek black shape of the Silencer Mk. 6, its claws finding purchase along the tiled floor as it turned and faced down the hall. Levvy and Sunny turned in horror to the thing sprinting towards them, Sunny calling out a warning.

Levvy gasped.

All of a sudden, gravity returned to Xal as though some giant hand had closed around their body and given a mighty *yank*. They plummeted past James, past Sylvia, all the way down, and had Shui not thrown himself desperately at the gap to snag Xal's wrists as they fell by, they might've hit the bottom. Shui's ribs *crunched* as he was dragged flat against the floor by Xal's weight, and Xal's vision flickered in and out as they came to a very sudden stop. They couldn't see. They couldn't *breathe.* It was as though every bone in their body, every bruised muscle, hell, even their busted brain had been cracked like a whip, and the tendons in their shoulders were threatening to give.

Above them, Levvy had turned away from the Silencer and leaped the gap, aiming with all her desperation towards the outstretched arms of James, hand in her mouth, spell in her mind –

But she was out of breath. With nothing left to give the spell, Levvy fell like a stone, her outstretched hand slipping through James's, body falling past Sylvia, past Shui and Xal, with no wind in her left for a final scream. James's mouth hung open, his eyes wide and staring all the way until Levvy plummeted out of sight. All four spell-lights were snuffed out of existence, plunging everyone into darkness.

" – al! *Xal*!" The words slipped back into Xal's battered mind. Shui's hold around their wrists was shaking. "*Don't pass out! Doc, help me!*" They felt more hands reach down to grip their arms but with less surety than the two already holding them.

Sunny dove over the side right as the Silencer pounced, but instead of attempting the same leap Levvy had failed, she clung to the edge and swung below to the floor just beneath her. The Silencer paid her no mind and continued on with its target – James. It struck him clean in the chest, claws puncturing leather and flesh indiscriminately as it bowled him over. He cracked his head against the floor, holding the creature back solely by his legs bowed up against his chest and a hand pressed against its sternum, while his other arm shielded his head in a desperate attempt at cover. "Doc! Shoot it!"

"I'm – ! A little busy here!" Alonzo snapped back. Xal was just about over the lip of the hole. With one last mighty pull, they cleared it, left flat on the floor like a discarded toy. Shui immediately curled in around his ribs, breathing through the agony.

Sunny's grip on the lip of the hole slipped out of her fingers, and she screamed as she fell a story before landing hard on the next floor down, directly onto her wrist. The Silencer's head snapped up at the scream, twisting unnaturally around to look backwards at her. It was the opening James needed. He pushed with all his might, shoving the construct off him and into the pit. It snagged a hold of his leg, however, dragging him over with it even as he clung desperately to rubble and debris and finally the edge. "*Alonzo*!" he screamed again.

Alonzo scrambled to his feet, moving around the hole to get a better aim – and paused, eyes wide and glassy and full of wonder at the construct.

"It's hardly even scratched," he wondered aloud. "How has it stayed in such good condition?"

"You can figure it out when it's dead!" James yelled, holding on with all his might.

The mortal danger of his hired muscle snapped Alonzo out of his daze, and he fired three shots with Xal's gun – the first seared in front of the construct's visor to blast the ceiling beyond it. The second struck it in what could generously be called its thigh. The third caught it full in the face as it turned and leaped towards Alonzo, shorting out its trajectory and causing it to miss its mark, *thunk* against the edge, and fall into the darkness below. The echoing fall seemed to last for years, and while it weren't even close to that in actuality, it lasted for longer than echoes had any right to. The lab was *long*, and *deep*, and for the first time that realization seemed to cement itself in everyone's mind. When the quiet horror had released its hold on the small group, they moved with a silent efficiency down towards the floor with Xal, Shui, and Alonzo, and through the nearest set of doors. The moment everyone was through, James toppled an ancient filing cabinet in front of the door, then began piling whatever else he could find, desperation bleeding through every movement and every extra layer to the barricade.

"Lights!" he yelled. "Lights, damnit – !" James's voice broke with the realization that the only lights they had were the dim, red emergency lights that flickered in the hallway. His eyes widened in horror, then sunk closed. He pinched the bridge of his nose, and slumped against the barricade.

"I don't suppose either of y'all are spellslingers?" Sylvia asked, looking away.

"Can remember a few tunes, can't whistle for shit," Xal said from where they'd been dumped against the wall. Sunny shook her head.

For a moment no one spoke, each in their own state of revelation that they were all now, truly, in the darkness of the lab without Levvy. Sylvia returned to the barricade efforts, quietly encouraging James to do the same. Shui made no effort to join in whatsoever.

"Don't look at me like that," James snapped, bristling. "She slipped! There was nothing I could've – !" He cut himself off, turning away and focusing on the barricade. Shui said nothing, but his glare never wavered.

Sunny crouched down next to Xal. "How are you holding up?" she asked quietly.

Xal sucked in a breath between their teeth, but the gaze they leveled at Sunny was the most alert she'd seen in an hour. "Can't say I wanna do that again anytime soon," they said, giving an exhausted, breathy chuckle. They nodded towards Sunny. "How's your wrist?"

Sunny straightened back to standing, pulling her wrist farther out of eyesight. "It's fine," she said, too quickly.

Xal frowned. "I heard when you landed. Didn't sound pretty."

"Xal, drop it," Sunny snapped.

Xal's frown deepened, but before they could say anything, Alonzo strode over to snatch Sunny's wrist. "What are you hiding, you little – "

Alonzo's eyes widened, and he dropped her wrist like a hot plate. Sunny snatched her arm back, covering it once again with her other hand, her eyes just as wide and startled as Alonzo's.

"It's not what you think," she whispered desperately.

"No?" Alonzo's expression had shifted from shock to pure hunger. "And what should I be thinking, Miss Quill?"

Sunny shook her head. She took a step back. Alonzo took a step forward, putting him in front of Xal.

Xal's eyes were on their guns.

"Sunny, that's an interesting designation, isn't it? I never took Dr. Quill as a sentimental man."

"*It's my name.*"

James and Sylvia were occupied with the door. Shui was injured. Alonzo was focused on Sunny. If they were going to get their guns, it had to be *now*.

"I always wondered where Dr. Quill found you, why he suddenly showed interest in becoming a family man instead of just hiring you on as an assistant."

They just had to get there first. Xal summoned whatever strength they had left, sliding their knees towards their chest. They were sweating, face pale, limbs shaking, but they pushed through with all they had. This was their shot –

"Doc!" The opportunity slipped through their hands just as Levvy had slipped through James's, as James and Sylvia finished with the barricade, both still clearly wound with restless energy. "I don't know how well that'll hold, we gotta get going ... " James paused, glancing between Alonzo and Sunny, who shrank even further from view. "Am I interrupting something?"

Alonzo leveled one last, long glance at Sunny. Sunny pulled the sleeve of her coveralls so far down it nearly covered her fingertips.

"Not a thing," he said, his eyes still sparkling with hunger. "Not a single thing."

4

— ◆ —

Now, Xal's brain wasn't one for numbers even before the bullet, but they could feel their body making the calculations their brain didn't care to. Though they kept their weight on Sylvia, they could feel control over their legs finally turning into something useful. Maybe not consistent, but a bullet only needs to strike true once.

Shui was injured; it was clear from the way he walked he'd busted his ribs something fierce. His standing within the group seemed equally rocky; the argument he'd had with James seemed as though it weren't the first by far, and the tension had only gotten worse with the loss of Levvy. He seemed intent to burn a hole in James's skull with his glare alone, hands gripping his rifle with a force they did not need. With the numbers they'd first come down with, Xal wouldn't have had a chance. But then, they didn't have the numbers anymore, now did they? And while it was difficult to quantify a human life as being more or less obtrusive to their survival, with the bandits' spellslinger out of the way, their chances had gone up significantly. The original pack of six had dwindled down to three, not counting Alonzo. Truly, Alonzo hardly registered on Xal's radar; the man couldn't shoot for shit and was clearly unliked by his hirelings, and money would only stave off starving dogs for so long. If they could somehow force the issue, they could get a chance to skedaddle while the rest tore each other apart.

'Course, much of that plan relied on Xal getting their guns back and Sunny working with them, not against them. The first part was doable. Alonzo had them and couldn't hit nothing with them. Were it a fair fight, they would trounce him no problem. Of course, with the bullet to the brain, it was going to be an unfair fight no matter what, so they were gonna have to keep an eye out for some way to tip the scales in their favor.

Sunny ... Sunny was a problem. They could feel their plans and calculations stutter to a halt every time Sunny was thrown into the picture. She'd hired them, but beyond that, there was nothing. No reason they were down in the lab, no reason she was so insistent on reaching the bottom, nothing to explain whatever history or tension there was between herself and Alonzo beyond whatever history Alonzo had with Dr. Quill, and Xal hadn't caught a glimpse of whatever it was that Alonzo saw. She was hiding something, and Xal wasn't sure if she was hiding it from just Alonzo and his dogs or from Xal as well.

Xal didn't like not knowing, but then, at the same time, not knowing felt about as familiar as anything else, so they supposed they may as well make peace with this as well.

Alonzo had eyes only for Sunny. Even with their suspicions, it still set a knot tightening in Xal's stomach the way Alonzo looked at her as though she were a thing. Their brain may have been full of quite literal holes, but they knew nothing good ever came from looks like that. Sunny, for her part, dutifully ignored him or, at the very least, made her best attempt.

As such, despite Sunny and Alonzo being in the front of the group, with Sunny's eyes on the floor and Alonzo's eyes on Sunny, and Xal's eyes on Alonzo and Shui's eyes on James, it was James who spotted it first.

"Doc, hold up," he said, pausing mid-stride and peering through the cracked glass of one of the larger windows along the hall. Parts of the building had been shaken to pieces this far down, either by the Shattering or the afterquakes or the regular, non-apocalyptic earthquakes, or just from a burrower digging through a load-bearing wall. The red lights flickered and spat, casting most of the floor into shadow that left folks blind in a way they'd never been with Levvy's lights. Most of the rooms they had passed so far were the same as those higher up, offices filled with monitors and pieces of equipment.

"What?" Alonzo snapped.

"You're gonna want to take a look at this."

"If this is more long-broken tech, then I have already made myself clear – " Alonzo stopped mid-sentence as he caught a glimpse of what James had spotted: another construct, though bulkier than the one that had attacked them. Unlike the Silencer, this one was motionless, still strapped into some kind of dock as though merely asleep.

"Do you think it's alive, like the other one?" Sylvia asked, her voice barely above a whisper.

"They're not *alive*," Alonzo corrected, staring intently at the new construct. "They're merely pretending to be. A facsimile, that's all. Isn't that right, Sunny?"

Sunny refused to meet his eyes. Alonzo eyed her for a long moment before moving towards the doors to the chamber. "Well, in that case, if our resident construct expert has nothing to add, we should go investigate, hm?"

" ... I thought Xal was the expert?" Shui said.

All eyes turned towards Xal, still slung over Sylvia's shoulder. For their part, they were staring through the fogged glass, squinting and trying to get a better view of the thing before speaking up. "Don't think this one ever made it to market," they commented.

"All the more reason to investigate," Alonzo said cheerfully.

"Wait – we shouldn't – " Sunny seemed to war with herself before she ran after Alonzo. "Leave it alone!"

"Don't worry, as long as no one touches anything, I'm sure nothing will happen." The doors had been covered in debris, but there was a small enough gap for Alonzo to squeeze into the room. Dread began to pool in Xal's stomach.

"He's lost it," Shui muttered, only to get cuffed on the head as James passed by. For a moment Shui stood still, a dangerous set to his shoulders, glaring at James's back, and only once Sylvia and Xal had squeezed in did he enter the room.

It was difficult to see in the dim light, but the chamber they entered was larger than the ones they'd seen thus far. Desks and broken-down monitors surrounded the looming figure of the construct docked in the center of the room. Thick wires and tubing shot off away from the dock back to the monitors and beyond, like the roots of some twisted tree. The slumbering beast was easily several feet taller than any of them, and twice as wide as even James. The rest of the group kept their distance, but Alonzo strode purposefully up to the construct with Sunny hot on his heels.

"Alonzo, *stop*!" Sunny yelled, only to flinch back as he turned on her.

"Why, feeling some kind of kinship with it, are we?" he asked, stepping forward. "You know, Sunny, your father never did say what he found at the first lab."

"I-I told you earlier." Sunny took a stumbling step back. "Just some broken experimental constructs and references to this lab. That's all."

Shui shook his head and turned away, but James and Sylvia watched the argument with rapt attention. "And – remind me, Sunny, dear." Alonzo took another step forward. "What exactly brought you down here?"

"I'm a scrapper. It's my *job*." But she no longer sounded as sure of herself as she once had. "I – "

Whatever Sunny had been about to say was lost as she tripped backwards over one of the thick wires. She crashed to the ground, hard – and from one of her pockets skittered a single, complex crystal lattice glowing a pale blue against the darkness of the floor. Alonzo stopped, staring. Sunny froze as well, eyes wide. The lattice was clearly modern – clunky and unwieldy in comparison to the ancient lattices they'd already seen that day – but for a modern lattice it was shockingly intricate. The frame was two concentric overlapping triangles all hooked into one another, the blue crystals shimmering and pointing in a spiral as they wrapped around the frame, the shape of the entire thing wholly unfamiliar to everyone in the room but Sunny.

"What ... is that?" Alonzo asked, low and dangerous.

Sunny's eyes were wide and terrified. All the eyes in the room were on her. And as she opened her mouth to say something, *anything* – Xal made their move.

Xal stomped with all the weight and force they could muster down onto Sylvia's foot and felt bones give way under the heel of their boot. There was no time to revel in the strike; the moment Sylvia began to howl and curl in pain, they followed the motion and shoved her over their leg – and as she went sprawling, they snagged her gun.

They shot once – twice – the first bullet cracking against the control panel by James's arm, the second missing Alonzo's head by a hair. Sunny shoved Alonzo back into the construct and dove along the floor to snatch the crystal and shove it back in her pocket. James pointed his gun towards Xal, and Xal pointed Sylvia's gun right back and fired – only for the gun to click empty. They swore, ducked under James's shots, and flung the empty gun at him.

Sylvia's gun flew through the air in what could have been considered a perfect arc, dead-shot aim, eagle-eyed and one in a million, were it not for the fact that Xal's vision still had yet to fully clear and they'd been aiming for James, who hadn't hardly needed to dodge the gun as it sailed by and perfectly struck the control panel.

Brilliant blue sparks crackled along the ancient control systems, drowning out the red emergency lights and blinding the room's occupants. Xal dove behind one of the control panels, and Sunny rolled under another; James flinched back, and Sylvia curled up into a protective ball; Alonzo took a startled step away from the construct, and the construct *screamed*.

It was a horrible noise, one that was so irrefutably human but forced out of parts no human had, like a construction site trying to speak. The construct screamed and strained and Alonzo had barely enough time to draw Xal's gun before the construct had pulled its bonds up by the root and *slammed* a flailing arm the size of a tree trunk into his side. Doctor Alonzo Morris went flying, and Xal's gun went clattering to the ground.

Xal and Sylvia shared a single look before they both scrambled for the weapon. They reached the gun at the same time, wrestling for it as best they could while, in the center of the room, the construct freed another of its gargantuan limbs, screaming that same horrible, mechanical scream.

"Shut it down, *shut it down*!" James was yelling, trying to distract it from Shui who was desperately pressing random controls in the hopes that *something* would change. "Where the *fuck* is the scrapper?!"

On the ground, Sylvia held on with all her wiry might, even if she was half the size of Xal. "Give me the gun," she spat, "so I can shoot the damn thing!"

"Sorry," Xal grunted, "but I think I'd rather take my chances with *it*." Before they could stop to consider the consequences, Xal *slammed* their head into Sylvia's, knocking her skull against the concrete floor. Both of them lost dizzy seconds, but Xal swam back to the surface first, slotted their gun back perfectly into their hand, and fired.

No one could be quite sure where exactly they were aiming, but sunlight spat from the mouth of their gun to sheer past the construct and clip James through the thigh, filling the ancient air with the pungent smell of burning meat. James howled in pain at the same moment the construct screamed that same metal scream, hauling its legs out and away from where the bolt had burned its way across its armored shell. It reeled back, flailing its horrific arms along with the wires still stuck deep in it like IV lines, smashing controls and lattices and nearly Shui if he hadn't ducked and rolled and –

"XAL!" Sunny screamed.

Xal moved, but not fast enough. The flailing arm struck them like a meteor hits the atmosphere: brutal, merciless, and entirely unaware. They felt their bones move in a way bones should not move and their skeleton rattle through all the aftershocks, and they squeezed their eyes shut and braced for the impact they knew was coming.

"*XAL*!" Sunny screamed again as their body *smashed* into the far wall and crumpled boneless to the floor. Xal didn't respond, but the construct had turned to where they'd been flung and was advancing. There was enough intelligence in it to recognize the threat in the hand that wielded such a gun. There was no time to think. Sunny sprinted out from her hiding place, ducked around James and Shui, and snagged the gun from Xal's limp grip.

"*Stop*!" The gun shook in Sunny's small hands as she placed her tiny body between Xal's prone form and the looming figure of the construct.

The construct stopped.

Sunny's breath caught in her chest, eyes wide. The construct leaned forward but not as a threat – it was almost as though it were confused. Another horrible, garbled, twist-of-metal noise groaned from it, but instead of a scream, it was a question.

The gun rattled in Sunny's hands. "I said – "

Sunlight burst through the air and exploded across the back of the construct. It reeled back, screeching and screaming and turned on the shooter – Alonzo, who'd just barely picked himself up off the ground.

"Xal, *wake up.*" Sunny shook them by the shoulders. "*Xal.*" Their head flopped over, fresh blood once again dripping slowly from their forehead.

"Get them up." Sunny started as Shui spoke; she hadn't even heard him move. On the other side of the room the construct was still fighting with Alonzo, James, and Sylvia. "This is your chance, but we need to move *now.*" When Sunny didn't immediately move, Shui knelt down and hauled Xal up before shoving their dead weight back to her. "In the storage room there's a vent. Drag them if you have to, but this is the best chance you'll get."

Still, Sunny hesitated. "Why are you – ?"

"It don't matter none, now *go.*" Shui shoved them along, watching the fight in the room. James had begun yelling for him, a yell Shui was blatantly ignoring. Sunny spent only a second more before stowing Xal's gun in her coveralls and getting a move on. The storage room was filled top to bottom with pieces and parts of lattices and crystals and tools for activities Sunny couldn't even begin to imagine, all long since rusted or shattered or claimed by entropy in one way or another.

True to Shui's word, there was a vent near the floor, just large enough for the two of them. Sunny popped the cover, then looked back.

"I'll make sure they don't follow." Shui pulled a wicked-looking knife from his belt and began prying open the door controls. "Don't worry about me."

"Thank you," Sunny said, and from the look in his eyes, she didn't think anyone had told him that in a very long time.

"Stop wasting time," he snapped instead, already prying off the casing to the control panel. "Get going already."

Sunny steeled herself, took a breath, and hauled Xal into the darkness.

5

There was no light in the vents. After a few twists and turns while dragging Xal backwards into the unknown, the red emergency lights and the odd flash of gunfire no longer reached Sunny. Not that it mattered. There was no real way for her to both see where she was headed and take Xal along easily. Time stretched and distorted with nothing to see; all sounds were garbled and echoed and blended into the natural groans of the ancient structure. There were times where her eyes would play tricks on her in the darkness, where out of the corner of her eye she would catch sight of some soft glowing emanating from the bloodied plane of Xal's forehead – but when she would turn to look, there would be nothing, only darkness.

"Xal," she said, not for the first time. "Xal, you need to wake up."

Xal didn't so much as twitch. Sunny was tempted to search for a pulse, but then she'd seen them get back up from a bullet to the brain, so she dutifully ignored the way their bones seemed to shift and move in ways they shouldn't. They were alive. They had to be alive. If they weren't alive, if Sunny had just been dragging a corpse down who knew how many vents –

"*Xal*," she called again, desperately trying to pull herself out of her spiraling thoughts. "Xal, *please*."

Sunny had never liked the darkness. She hated being alone, and loathed feeling helpless most of all. She'd fallen into a routine by this point, a muscle memory loop of dragging Xal deeper and deeper down, and as the loop became rote it freed her mind up to think and dwell.

"If I ever see Alonzo again," she growled, dragging Xal another length backwards, "I'm going to kill him. I don't give a shit if he was my dad's colleague, I don't *care*. I'm going to shoot him, but I'm a bad shot, so I need you awake to finish him off."

Silence.

"He's still got your other gun, yeah?" she said, switching tactics. "You're real possessive about those, aint'cha? I ain't seen guns like that since – since – " Even with her charge unconscious and unhearing, Sunny couldn't bring herself to say it aloud. "They're unique, you ain't findin' shit like that in the Wastes, not in such good quality either. They're important to you." She dragged them back another length. "You wanna get it back, right? Can't do it like this."

Silence. Sunny's grip trembled, thoughts of pulses and brains splattering a cave wall swirling through her mind.

"Xal." Her voice was small. Almost inaudible. "Xal, you have to wake up." She tried to put more strength into the words, but her resolve cracked at the end. "Xal, *please* – "

Her voice broke at the same time the vent behind her dropped suddenly and dramatically, sending them both sliding down at a sharp angle. Sunny didn't have the breath for any more than a surprised gasp as they tumbled backwards for what felt like an eternity. Metal hit Sunny's back and nearly dislodged the sob she'd been desperately burying. She bit down, tried to hold it in with the force of her jaw strength. When that failed, she clamped both hands down across her mouth. She screwed her eyes shut and held on, scarcely bothering to breathe.

She could not break here.

She would not break here.

There was still so much else she needed to get done.

She held herself there, submerged in that breathless state until her systems alerted her to the need to breathe. She held a second or two longer, just to remember what it felt like to hold her breath, and opened her eyes.

Xal still had not moved from where they lay, sprawled on her lap. She held the disappointment and let it wash away. She took the advantage laying on the ground had granted her and looked ahead.

Ahead of her, there was faint red light slipping in through the slats on the bottom of the vent. To the right of her, sitting in an offshoot of the vents that went deeper into the building, the Silencer Mk. 6 stared back.

Sunny's eyes went wide. She froze like a mouse in sight of a hawk and pulled Xal's body protectively closer. The Silencer was crouched on what could generously be called the tips of its fingers and toes, almost invisible in the darkness save for the faint red light reflecting off its black chassis. Sunny didn't move, couldn't move, Xal's gun in her coveralls too buried to be of any use. The construct moved too fast; there would be no way for her to get it in time.

The two stared each other down for what felt like an eternity, every fiber of Sunny tensed to move the moment *it* did –

The construct slipped further into the darkness and crawled silently away deeper into the vents.

Sunny's breath left her in a *woosh*, and she let her head fall back to the vent in horrid, confused relief. It should have ended her. It should have killed her the way it had already killed three people. She should be –

She closed her eyes and counted down. Thought of all the ways one could dismantle an ancient lattice. Mentally organized all of the tools waiting for her at her workbench back home. Looked back down at the body in her arms. It didn't matter why they hadn't been torn apart, she would have to take her gifts where they were.

"I'll be right back, okay?" she said, patting Xal on the shoulder as she disentangled herself from them and peered through the vent cover. It was hard to tell how far down the floor was, and it would be nearly impossible to close the hatch back up to hide their tracks, but Sunny was tired of dragging Xal through the darkness. It was worth the risk.

Sunny got to work prying open the vent cover. After everything else she had dealt with so far, the action was refreshingly mundane. It was held closed only by a few screws, which came loose easily under her deft hands.

When she looked down to the room below, it was difficult to say just how far the drop would be. She would be fine, she'd dealt with harder falls than this, but Xal had yet to wake up. She looked at their prone body guiltily a moment longer before pulling herself together. They didn't have a choice.

"I'm sorry," Sunny said, hooking her arms back under Xal's and dragging them into position. "I wish I didn't have to, but – but you'll be okay, alright? You survived being shot in the head, you survived that construct rearranging your skeleton, you'll survive a fall like this." She breathed in, steeling herself in their stead. "Okay. Okay. Let's go." She pulled their leather duster off their limp frame and dropped it to the ground below, figuring that any cushion she could provide would be better than no cushion at all.

Xal dropped like a doll, all floppy limbs and ligaments, but by some miracle they didn't seem to hurt themself any worse than they already had.

After a second of steeling herself, Sunny followed suit, dropping and rolling and hearing something clatter and skitter away while she caught her breath. Then her brain caught up with her ears and she patted down the many pockets of her coveralls before her gray eyes flew wide and scanned the floor – there! The crystal lattice she'd so jealously guarded had escaped again, rolling to a halt at the center of the room.

Sunny scrambled to pick it up, turning it over to search for cracks or blemishes or any possible sign of damage. The crystal lattice remained intact. She clutched it to her chest and screwed her eyes shut.

When she opened them, she got her first real look at the room. It was similar to the room they had just left, control panels and office chairs and fractured lattices and wires thick enough to be vines all in similar places – and in the center of it all was a chair. A padded chair, raised slightly from the ground, with leather straps at the arm rests. Every single part of the chair was adjustable, from the footrest to the headrest, all able to move to fit a wide range of bodies. Able to fit perfectly around a girl, just barely an adult, thin and sick.

There are as many ways a brain can react to something awful as there are brains. Some burrow deep in the pain, make a nest of it and then turn that nest into a fortress, letting no one in or out. Others turn it into a weapon, sharpen it over years so that they could hurt others before hurt could be done to them once more. Some carry that pain, learn to live with it, learn to love with it. Others just drown.

Sunny had done what a nontrivial amount of folks do and buried her pain so deep she couldn't even begin to think about it with any kind of clarity, only able to conceive of it in the abstract as though it had happened to someone else. See, the problem with this method is that pain don't forget – and all it took to bring the abstract into sharp relief was to get a glimpse, a reminder of the real thing.

The straps around her wrists were strong, well-made, and didn't allow her to move an inch. She couldn't try if she wanted to – weak, sick, in so much pain she almost couldn't wait for it to be over. The overhead lights burned her sensitive eyes, but she couldn't flinch away. Her breath caught in her throat and held there, even as they turned the horrid machine on – and the tugging, the extraction, the taffy-pull of something untouchable being wrenched piece by piece away from her physical form, torn away from tendons and sinew and nerve endings all the same – she screamed, she knew she screamed, but no one could hear her, or no one *cared* to hear her –

And then she was spun like thread into wires and cables and something cold and unforgiving with only a fractal understanding of what her life had been, and what it was now.

Sunny was pulled back into the present with a gasp as noise echoed down the vents. Her breathing sped to a breakneck pace and did not slow, and the hands that pulled Xal's gun from her coveralls shook like the Shattering itself.

"Sunny? Are you – "

Sunny fired, her shot going wild and blasting into the metal of the vents. Shui lost his grip and dropped to the floor in surprise, landing gracelessly among the debris. "*Sunny*! Don't – Fuck, don't shoot, I'm not here to hurt you!"

"No, you're just here to take me back to people who will!" Sunny yelled back, not moving her shaky aim from where Shui had landed.

"I left them back there," Shui said, calmly and slowly. His hands were in the air; he hadn't moved from where he'd fallen. "If they're still alive, they'll have to find a different way down."

"Why should I believe you?" Sunny's grip on the gun wasn't quite as strong as it had been.

"Because they're a bunch of idiots who are going to get themselves killed, and I'm done pretending they won't." Slowly, Shui moved from the ground to his knees. When he wasn't blasted to pieces, he began moving slowly closer. "I wanna live. And I'm guessing you do too."

"You know *nothing* about me."

Shui stilled, certain he'd crossed a line. The seconds ticked by, and he remained un-shot. "You're right, I don't." He was close enough now that he could reach out and grab the gun itself if he wanted. "But I do know that out here, rates of survival tend to be higher the larger the group. And, not for nothin', but with your gunslinger the way they are, I don't know how much help you're getting."

"Their name's Xal," Sunny corrected miserably. Shui's hands rested on her own, not forcing, just asking.

"Put the gun down, Sunny," Shui said. "Please."

He covered her vision, obscuring the hateful chair and the rest of the lab. For a moment, Sunny could almost pretend that they were in any other room in the ruins, lit only by the dim emergency lights. She squeezed her eyes shut, pulling herself back piece by piece. Not here. Not now. She lowered the gun. Shui's relief bled through his fingertips as he pulled away – and froze.

Sunny opened her eyes and followed his gaze. The sleeve of her coveralls had slid down, exposing her wrist. On the back of her forearm, where she'd landed hard, the dermal layer covering her body had split open. There was no blood, no open wound to risk infection, merely synthetic skin peeling back to reveal the metal of her body.

Sunny flinched back, finding her escape blocked by one of the consoles. Shui's eyes were wide, but, unlike Alonzo, Shui looked rightly horrified. Sunny rolled her sleeve back down as best she could without letting go of the gun.

Shui merely stared as his brain tried to figure out what exactly was the appropriate response. " ... Does Xal know?" he asked, finally.

"No one knows," Sunny whispered. "Are you serious about this? About helping get us out of here?"

If Shui was surprised by the sudden resolve, he didn't say anything about it. "Yes."

Sunny nodded and finally put away the gun. "Then help me get them out."

Xal, still sprawled out cold where they landed, said nothing.

Sunny kept her eyes anywhere but the center of the room as the two of them struggled through hoisting Xal's duster back on them, and then hoisting Xal onto their shoulders. Shui had originally attempted to muscle through the act himself, but his ribs had all too quickly decided they were not up to task. She had a fleeting thought of how none of them had gotten through this unscathed, followed by an unfortunate thought of just how far they had yet to go. Down in the depths of the lab, the emergency lights held even less power, barely illuminating a foot around where they were embedded in the ceiling, some dead completely. It was such that when Sunny produced the map from her pocket, the pink light nearly blinded the both of them.

"I thought Dr. Morris had that?" Shui commented.

"He did before I snagged it." Sunny paused a moment, analyzing the projected light. "Alright, I think we're about ... here." She chewed at her lip, thinking. "I doubt we'll have any luck with the stairs, and without a spellslinger, there's no way we can pull that stunt that took us down again, but maybe we could scale the elevator shaft? See if we can't haul Xal up after us?"

"What about the Silencer?" Shui asked.

Sunny turned her encounter with the construct over in her mind. "We ain't seen it since," she said finally. "It might be safe to say it's more interested in Alonzo and the others. Elevator's still our best bet."

Shui had half a mind to point out to her that the Silencer was able to climb walls and had hunted them through the vents and they were likely to be easy pickin's no matter *which* vertical shaft they attempted to climb, should the construct chance upon them again. Sunny, however, had begun moving them down the hall as though the argument had been solved one way or the other.

According to the map they were roughly two-thirds of the way to the bottom. Despite knowing it was theoretically possible to go even deeper, the bowels of the earth made themselves known in the darkened underground halls. The walls seemed to press in on them, the air heavy and forceful like water at the depths of the ocean. Despite this, despite the almost humid feeling of the earth, it had become increasingly frigid the further down they'd gone. Where once there might have been climate-spells woven into the rest of the building, now it was bereft and subjugated to the whims of the rocks so far away from the sun.

Shui shivered, not wanting to dwell too much on just how deep they were.

"Not too far now," Sunny said. "Then we can get you two back to the surface."

Shui frowned, something in her phrasing tickling the back of his mind but nothing more. On his shoulders, Xal twitched. Just a hand at first, but the movement traveled up their arm into their shoulder.

"Xal?" Shui called. Xal didn't respond, but they did twitch again. "Sunny, I think they're waking up."

Sunny paused, but her eyes were on the end of the hallway that was lost in darkness. They lowered Xal as gently as they could against the wall. The twitching was stronger now – not quite spasms but something more intentional. Their eyes went from peacefully closed to screwed shut in concentration as their chest bowed forward, then side to side. There was a series of horrifying cracks and pops as their skeleton forced its way back into place. Xal let out a groan that was half agony, half relief, before opening a bleary pale eye.

"'D'ja see the ship that hit me?" they slurred.

"*What*?" Shui asked.

"What?" Xal responded, equally confused. Shui shook his head, setting aside the millions of questions he had for the task of checking the rest of Xal over. Xal frowned as Shui checked the bullet hole; it had scabbed over, but if he squinted, there was almost an afterglow to the dried blood on their forehead. "Ain't you one of them folks that kidnapped us?" they slurred.

"Not anymore," Shui said, checking their neck.

"That's good." Their speech was getting better by the second, which meant whatever blow they'd taken hadn't been *too* bad. Or, at least, it wasn't any longer. They groaned again, their hands moving to their empty holsters by their sides. "... Thought I'd grabbed one of my guns." They swore under their breath and knocked their head back against the wall in frustration.

"Sunny has it. Sunny – " Shui turned down the hall to call her over, but when he looked, she was already running headlong into the darkness. "Sunny, what the hell – ?!"

The light from the map illuminated her path as she sprinted, all the way up to the partially crumbled door to the elevator with a hole just wide enough for her to slip through.

"Damnit, Sunny!" Xal was up and moving with shocking speed for someone who had just reset their spine. They ran with the most sure footing they'd had in the last few hours, which wasn't saying much, but did mean they weren't too far behind her.

"Go back to the surface!" she yelled from the elevator shaft. Something else groaned underneath her, ancient and metallic. "This ain't your problem!"

"Like hell it ain't – " Xal stopped against the crack in the door, heaving for breath even after the short run. "I may not know why you hired me, but I *know* you hired me and I ain't leaving you down here in the dark – !" With a last burst of effort, Xal squeezed their way through and tumbled down through the darkness to land on the ancient elevator car next to her. The car groaned again, louder this time but just as ignored by the folks sitting on top of it.

"I'm serious, Xal," Sunny warned. "I hired you and now I'm telling you to *go back to the surface*. End of contract, go back to your raptor and *leave me alone*."

"*You still have my gun* – !" Xal spluttered as Sunny threw it at them. "Fine, *Alonzo* has my other gun."

"Who cares about your guns?!"

"I care about my guns!"

"Xal, they already shot you in the head!"

The indignant squeak Sunny made when Xal rolled their eyes damn near reached dog pitches.

"*One time*, and if anything, that should be reason enough to keep me along."

"*Folks*," Shui called from above, hanging off the entrance. "This ain't the time or place, simmer down and let's talk this – *oop* – "

Shui slipped, and fell, and thudded onto the ancient elevator car, which had weathered all the quakes and aftershakes of the Shattering and all the centuries after but was drawing the line at three adult bodies. The trio had just enough time to hold on before the elevator car began moving – slowly at first with a bone-breaking groan, then fast as lightning plummeting to the depths below, sending them all crashing into absolute darkness.

6

It was dark at the bottom. At least, Xal hoped they were at the bottom. The idea that at any moment they could plummet down who knew how many more floors was an unpleasant one. The alarms had stopped working altogether this far down. In the distance above them Xal could faintly see red light flickering in through the elevator doorways. The only sound was the echoing groans of the ruins. When it was clear they were in no immediate danger of plummeting further, Xal shifted and groaned.

"Shui?" they called. "You alive?"

"Close enough," Shui grumbled, shifting as well. The sounds of fabric and leather and the metal of his rifle clanging against the metal of the elevator car was somewhere off behind and to Xal's left.

"Sunny?" There was no immediate answer. "Sunny, you there?"

A choked-back sob broke through the quiet before it was wrangled back to something more manageable. Xal felt their heart break a little. They followed the sound to its source, where Sunny lay curled up on her side, crying silently with all she was worth.

"I'm sorry," she managed between sobs. "I didn't mean to."

"Aw, Sunny." Xal sat down next to her and placed a hand on her shoulder. "Sorry I yelled."

"I'm just so *tired* of all of it," she sniffed. "I'm tired of Alonzo, I'm tired of you dying, I'm tired of these *stupid fucking labs*. It's been hundreds of years, it shouldn't matter anymore."

Now, Xal wasn't particularly versed in conversation – their attention span was shit and they were adept at saying not necessarily the *wrong* thing, but somethin' that certainly weren't the right – but even they knew sometimes you just had to let a fella talk. So they waited as Sunny cried herself back to a somewhat more even keel, then waited some more in the darkness and silence, listening to Shui shift nervously.

"I'm not a real person," Sunny said finally. It took every inch of willpower Xal had not to argue. The only thing that stopped them was the knowledge that if they stopped her now, Sunny might never start back up. "I'm ... " She pulled a hand down her face, wiping away tears and snot that simply didn't exist. "The 'Fore-Folks were developing things they shouldn't've, right up until it killed them. We know this. You've all seen it. But a decade before the Shattering, the big, new, shiny thing was constructs. The 'Fore-Folks made them more and more complicated for increasingly specialized jobs, but that took time and effort and so much intricate spellweaving that they started looking into easier ways to ... get results." Sunny paused, taking a breath. "So they started putting folks in them."

For a moment the elevator shaft was silent, before Shui shook his head. "No, no, that ain't possible – "

"Folks ain't even *begun* to unravel everything the 'Fore-Folks could do," Sunny said gravely. "But they made something that could pull" – her voice cracked, but she continued on nonetheless – "the soul out of – out of someone and attach it to something else. It was supposed to allow for more complicated constructs, but it just ... "

"So then, that room back there ... " Shui trailed off in horrified silence. Sunny nodded, even though no one could see. "And – and the constructs we've seen so far ... "

"They weren't supposed to go that far," Sunny said miserably. "It wasn't – I didn't think they would. I didn't think *he'd* sign off on it."

Xal and Shui exchanged a glance. "Didn't think *who* would sign off on it?" Xal asked.

"It doesn't matter," Sunny said, too quickly. It was a longer pause this time before the words could be pulled out of her. "It was the lead researcher's daughter. They – " Sunny swallowed the words in her throat and thought more on them before continuing. "She was sick. Dying. So they made her the prototype, made a whole replacement body to put her in just to see if it would work, but the process – it scrambles you. It wasn't perfect." The bitterness that had crept into her voice was nearly all-encompassing now. "But I guess that didn't matter much, considering the kind of bodies they were making down here. Didn't matter much whether the person was whole or fractured if they're just making a weapon that can *think*." Her hands came up and slowly covered her face, gripping her short hair. "I'm so *stupid*. I should've known that they wouldn't stop with ... " Even now, even after saying everything else out loud, she still couldn't say it. The truth held itself in her mouth like a rock someone else had placed there, weighty and unmoving and waiting for her to choke.

"Aw, Sunny," Xal said quietly. She closed her eyes, held them shut.

"You're a 'Fore-Folk," Shui said – just as quietly as Xal had, but it was as though he'd shouted the words in her ear. Sunny's eyes snapped open and she sat up, glaring at him.

"A *real* 'Fore-Folk wouldn't have a fake body!" she yelled. "I ain't her, I can't *be* her, I'm just – I'm just a scrambled up *ghost* in a body someone else put me in!"

"Sorry, sorry." Shui backed down.

"You *don't* know what it's *like*," Sunny continued. "I was scrambled up *before* they shoved me in stasis. I could hardly remember who I was half the time or how I was supposed to act, only that my body was *wrong*, that *I* was wrong, that I'd been given this beautiful second chance at life and I'd *fucked it all up*. And now – " She slammed her fist down against the roof of the elevator car, the dull *thud* echoing around the elevator shaft. "And now I find out hundreds of years later that they didn't stop with me, they took all of that and kept *hurting* people the same way they hurt me, and it doesn't even *matter* anymore because they all blew themselves up anyways but I still have to live with the fact that my father – that my father – " She covered her face in her hands and *breathed*.

Xal sighed and snapped their fingers in frustration. "Shoot, that means you were asleep during it."

For a moment Sunny was lost in the tonal whiplash. " … What?"

"The Shattering. No front-row primary source to the end of the world. Shame." Xal said it so casually, like they were disappointed in something trivial like losing at cards or missing a train, that Sunny couldn't help herself. A giggle snorted its way out of her.

"Sorry," she said, "'fraid I slept right through it."

"That's all – well, shit, this is a *lot* to absorb," Shui said, apparently the only one of the three to truly appreciate the enormity of what Sunny had just confessed. "But that don't explain why you'd want to come here."

"Or why you're so insistent on *not* going back to the surface," Xal grumbled.

"We weren't hunting you. Dr. Morris was shocked to find you here. I can't imagine why you'd want to go back to somewhere like this so badly."

"Does it have something to do with that lattice?" Xal prompted after a bit.

When Sunny spoke, weariness bled into her words. "When Dr. Quill uncovered the original lab and what was inside it, he became fixated on immortality. Started trying to figure out if he could do to himself what they'd done to – what they'd done. Started trying to recreate the tech, but he didn't have much to go on, didn't have any idea what he was doing. Eventually, though, he got *somewhere* ... " She reached into her coveralls, pulled out the lattice, and held it in the air. A gentle glow emanated from it, illuminating the darkness with a soft blue light. "He copied himself into this, and said that if something were to happen to him, he wanted to be – to be put in a construct, if there were any left whole that could be found. He wanted *me* to plug him in. Made me promise." Her fingers tightened around the crystal and she held it to her chest. "Two weeks later, he died."

The elevator shaft was quiet for some time, each person absorbing the information as best they could.

"Hell of a last request," Shui said, breaking the silence.

"He took care of me. He gave me a home when mine was ... gone. He woke me up, he could have been so much worse to me. Could've done whatever Alonzo will do if he gets his hands on me. How can I say no to that?" Her voice was small at the end, the last question not entirely rhetorical. Shui wanted to answer her in some way, but he held his tongue. He understood the way loyalty chained folks to one another and left them unable to stray from the path set out by someone else, no matter how dangerous.

Xal gave a big sigh and sat up. "Welp, you've still got my help," they said easily, as though none of this were particularly out of the ordinary. "I'm still missing a gun, and I've been itching for payback for the hole in my skull."

"Listen – " Shui started haltingly, unsure of how exactly to ask. "How *did* you survive that?"

"Survive what?"

"The bullet to the brain?"

"That was hours ago." Xal waved their hand dismissively.

"Xal, you *should* be dead," Sunny said patiently.

"I don't want to hear that from a *ghost*."

Realization hit Shui like a train. "You don't know," he said.

"Know what?"

"You have *no* idea why you aren't dead," Shui said again.

Xal shifted uncomfortably. "Listen, it just ain't that important." Sunny spluttered in the background. "I know my name. I know how to shoot." Xal took out their pistol, the inner fission radiating light dizzyingly on the walls as they spun it and re-holstered it. "And I know that Alonzo fella's a bastard who won't know what hit 'im. That good enough for y'all, or am I gonna have to sit through another hour of 'I don't know's?"

Sunny and Shui looked at each other, then back at Xal. "Yeah, I can work with that," Sunny said. "Shui?"

Shui breathed out a long sigh. "Well, I ain't climbing all the way out of here by myself. 'Sides, might as well make sure James doesn't follow me out to try and make it even between us. Not his kind of even, anyways."

"Naw, if I gotta try and explain whatever's up with me, *you* can elaborate on what's going on between you and James," Xal said.

"Frankly, after 'literal ghost' and 'mystery immortality,' I think my story's a bit bland." When it was clear the other two were waiting for him to continue, Shui sighed and scrubbed a hand through his dark hair. "Ain't nothin' no one's ever heard before. Joined up with this pack years ago, when it was under different leadership. Different leadership had planned to make me something more, James took offense with both that and said different leadership. Different leadership had an unfortunate accident, James and I had a scuffle, James won."

"That's it?" Sunny asked.

"Up until about five minutes ago it felt like reason enough to be mad at someone." He paused, thinking. "And, frankly, I think it still is. James's already gotten the majority of them killed, might as well finish the job."

When Sunny smiled, it was with a stronger smile than she'd had in hours. "Thank you both." Shui looked away, embarrassed. Xal beamed back. "Alright, let's hope this works." She rummaged around in her coveralls and pulled out the map, blinding everyone once again in the process. Once she'd blinked the spots away from her vision, Sunny scanned through the projected light. "Let's hope we're at the bottom. Everything I learned about this site said that this was where they were building the constructs." Her hands trembled, and though she did not need to, she swallowed nonetheless. "If we're going to find an empty construct, this is our best bet."

The three nodded to one another, then got to work. The elevator car that had buckled under their weight was so crusted over in grime they almost missed the hatch and, in fact, felt right by it several times, before Sunny's clever fingers finally found the lip. The hard part over, it was mere moments before she had it open, sending rust and debris falling into the pitch-black car. Sunny went first, dropping to the ground experimentally and feeling about with her hands and feet before declaring it safe enough. Xal went second, Shui lowering them down by their wrists for Sunny to catch around the waist. Shui went last, landing solidly and efficiently.

The doors were crumpled beyond repair, and it took all three of them to wedge it open – and when it was barely an inch apart, some small bit of leftover power that had survived the end of the world must've sparked, because the doors slid the rest of the way open on their own, overbalancing the trio and sending them sprawling to the floor.

"Now, isn't this a wonderful gift."

Three heads snapped up. Three pairs of eyes met the muzzles of three guns aimed directly at them. Doctor Alonzo Morris, with one eye swollen horrifically and crusted blood smeared along the side of his jaw, sneered down at them. "I do just love when things go my way."

7

The miracle that occurred deep in the depths of the abandoned lab that day was not Shui switching sides. It was not Sunny telling her story to people who were uninterested in dismantling her to see how she worked. It wasn't even Xal surviving a bullet to the brain. No, the real miracle was that James, Alonzo, and Sylvia had survived long enough to point guns at the other three.

Any good wastelander knows the rule of "loyalty is king." Humans are social critters and do best by working together in whatever manner that is. The second part of that rule is that there is nothing more dangerous than a pissed-off coworker, no matter how close you were, and it was clear to anyone with eyes that the loyalty between those three was hanging on by a thread. Doctor Alonzo Morris would never know just how far the sunk cost fallacy had gone in preserving his life a little longer.

Of course, the third part of that rule is that there ain't nothing better for morale than a common enemy.

James didn't wait for the order to be given before he hauled Shui up by his shirt, twisted his arm behind him and *slammed* him against the wall. "Thought you were real clever locking us in with that construct, didn't you? Thought it would take care of your problems for you instead of dealing with us yourself?" There were fresh tears in James's clothes and leathers, the leg Xal had shot wrapped in a field bandage. "The problem with running from your fights is sometimes your fights've got legs."

"Frankly," Shui said gruffly, "I was expecting this particular fight to trip down a garbage chute – " He cut off with a grunt of pain as James twisted his arm up higher.

"I'm going to enjoy this," he growled in Shui's ear.

Sylvia didn't bother hauling Xal to their feet. She kicked their hat aside then placed her boot on top of their head. "One false move, cowboy, and we find out just how much damage that skull of yours can take," she warned.

"Couldn't move if I tried," Xal said. "Take it your foot's doing better – " They cut off as Sylvia began applying pressure.

"As for you, Miss Quill, I do hope you're done running." Alonzo smirked. "It would be a shame to damage your chassis." He gestured with the gun. Sunny rose to her feet slowly, eyes locked onto Alonzo.

"How'd you get past the construct?" she asked warily.

"There are very few things that survive a blast from something like this " –he gave Xal's gun an incredibly clumsy twirl– "directly to the crystal lattice."

Sunny's hands flew to her mouth in horror.

"Boy, you must tell me where you got these guns," Alonzo said, oblivious.

"I ain't a boy," Xal ground out, "and even if I remembered, can't say I'd be right interested in turning you loose on some poor gunsmith." At Alonzo's frown, Sylvia dug her heel into their head further.

"A conversation for later, then," Alonzo said.

"You have no idea what you've done," Sunny hissed.

"Worried about your fellow constructs?" Alonzo sniffed. At that, both Sylvia and James looked over at Sunny. "It had gone mad with decay. Putting it down was a mercy. Besides, there's still so much we can learn from its corpse."

"*You have no idea what you've done,*" Sunny repeated, louder this time. "You're just flailing around with tech you don't understand and consequences you can't even imagine! At any time, you could trigger the wrong lattice, the wrong ancient doomsday device, and melt someone, but as long as it ain't you, you couldn't give less of a shit!" Sunny's voice grew in pitch and volume, echoing off the dark walls. "No wonder you ain't had any reasonable contributions in the last ten years that weren't riding on my dad's coattails, you absolute dust-brained *idiot*! What could you have possibly imagined you'd find down here to make this all worth it?"

"That's the beauty of these jobs." Alonzo's voice shifted into a lower, more dangerous register. "I don't need to imagine, I just need to know what investors would purchase because they didn't know any better."

"That's it? That's all you have to say for yourself? Four people are *dead* because of you," Sunny whispered.

"And I'm not afraid to raise that number. Now." He held out a hand. "The map."

Now, folks are often surprised just how much you can see while on the floor, even if your head is under another person's boot. Debris that would be otherwise hidden, for example. Holes the little burrowers had left, even this far down. And, what folks least expect, the ceiling. And holes in the ceiling, left by eons of decay among other things.

"Y'all might consider moving," they said, largely to the ground. One pale eye looked skyward past Sylvia, even as she ground her boot into the flesh of their cheek.

"Quiet!" she snapped. "I will squash that head of yours, don't tempt me."

"Naw, alright then, don't mind me – " They broke off in a quiet, pained gasp as Sylvia pressed harder.

"You genuinely do not know how to shut up, do you?" she snarled. Xal continued to watch something behind her. "I'll bet every person who killed you did so to finally get some peace and quiet – "

The Silencer Mk. 6 struck much like it had the first time, clawed hands snapping down to snag the bandolier strung across Sylvia's body, only to miss and tear into the meat of her shoulders and haul her into the air screaming.

Alonzo turned and aimed and was close enough that he may have actually been able to hit the thing, but the moment his eyes were off her, Sunny ducked her head and shoved him off-balance to the ground. Sunny sprinted past him down the hall, the pink light of the map illuminating her path as she ran.

"Get back here!" Alonzo screeched and scrambled after her.

"Hey – !" Sylvia choked around her bandolier, legs flailing. "Don't just leave – !" Before she could finish her sentence, the Silencer had hauled her up and slammed her against the walls with a sickening *crunch*, again and again and again and again –

In one fluid motion Xal rolled onto their back and drew their pistol, and in the darkness of the hall the bolt from its mouth shone like the sun before it was extinguished in the bloody forehead of Sylvia.

"Sylvia?!" James turned to look, and his hold on Shui loosened, letting Shui break free and wrap his arm around James's throat.

"Shouldn't've turned your back on me," he muttered before sinking his knife into the meat of James's back over and over until the larger man finally stopped twitching. Shui let the body slump to the floor.

The two still alive looked back to the ceiling. The Silencer stared back. It dropped Sylvia's corpse with a wet *thud*. The two flinched back as it leaped from its hiding place, only for it to ignore them and speed down the hall instead on all fours, chasing the trail left by Sunny and Alonzo.

Sunny didn't have a plan. She'd never had a plan, were she being completely honest with herself, no plan beyond hiring some help and fulfilling Dr. Quill's final wishes along the way. Now, sprinting as fast as she could down the hallway, she kept one hand on the map and the other pulling debris and ancient filing cabinets down behind her to slow Alonzo down.

If she could just get to the manufacturing ward, it would all be over. It was an irrational thought, but one she clung to nonetheless. Just another step. Just another step.

She slowed down as she came to the large double doors separating her from her goal and wasted no time prying open the lattice. Alonzo's voice, yelling and swearing and gasping for breath, was becoming too close for comfort, and the moment the doors rumbled open wide enough for her to slip between, she was through.

Sunny stumbled out onto a catwalk suspended over even deeper darkness than she'd thought possible, her footsteps echoing around the cavernous room. Around her all manner of machines lay inert, armatures and tools and pieces of other constructs held suspended where they'd died. In the center, suspended at the end of the walkway, was the largest construct that had ever been created. Easily the size of a house or larger, the construct was humanoid in the same way the last two constructs had been humanoid: enough that a soul could inhabit it without too much confusion, but no closer. It was mostly completed, armored like a tank and kitted out with weaponry built into its limbs and back.

Sunny swallowed around her frantic heartbeat, an echo of the biological impulses she no longer had. She stumbled forward, forcing herself to analyze it, to make sure it was unfinished. If it was unfinished, then it was uninhabited. If it was uninhabited, then ...

Sunny hesitated, halfway across the catwalk, staring up at the partially built monstrosity before her. It chilled her to think that however it was the 'Fore-Folks had destroyed themselves, they hadn't even gotten to the point of deploying such a thing. She could no longer sweat, but the hand clenched around the crystal lattice was cold and clammy all the same.

A bolt of sunlight cast horrific shadows on the walls of the room as it fizzed past Sunny and struck the railing, leaving it red-hot and smoldering.

"Nowhere to run, *construct*," Alonzo wheezed, aiming Xal's gun down the walkway. "It doesn't have to end this way. We could work together, you and I. You'll need someone on the surface to keep other scrappers and investors off your tail. I can be very ... persuasive." He caught his breath then straightened up, a pained look on his face that Sunny didn't trust for a *second*. "I don't want to do this. Dr. Quill was my friend, and I know he cared for you."

Sunny screwed up her face in rage. "You don't even think we're people!" she yelled. "We're just a meal ticket to you, you said it yourself!"

"Do you think Dr. Quill was any better?' Alonzo asked. "I respected that man, may his soul be at peace, but he was just as opportunistic as the rest of us. That's the only way anyone gets ahead out here. I'm sure whatever reason he sent you down here was *still* for his own gain, even now." Alonzo took a step forward, and Sunny backed away.

"Stop talking about him that way!" Sunny clenched the lattice tighter.

"He's not your father, and he's dead. Look around you! Look at what we could learn from this place, and from you! No one would ever have to go through the pain of losing a loved one ever again!" Alonzo threw his arms wide. "We could conquer death!"

"No one conquers death," Sunny whispered.

Alonzo smirked and looked as though he had more to say, but before he could, a sound echoed into the room through the doors and down the hall, the sound of metal slamming against concrete. Alonzo whirled behind him as the Silencer burst into the room and onto the walkway. He fired once – twice – three times. The first two were wide, the third sparking off the construct's shoulder. It didn't slow down.

The Silencer Mk. 6 sliced through Alonzo's chest with its claws, then snagged him by the arms and flung him like a ragdoll against the railing. Xal's gun went flying from Alonzo's grasp, and Sunny dove to keep it from clattering off the walkway.

"Stop – ! Please – !" Alonzo's pleas went unheeded as the Silencer rounded on him. He scrambled to his feet, running towards Sunny. "Sunny – !"

His words died in his mouth, his face frozen in shock as Sunny burned a hole through his gut from where she lay on the ground, hands steady around Xal's gun. Blood dribbled from his mouth as he tried to speak – only for the Silencer to snag him by the head and *slam* him against the ground. There was nothing left in him to resist as it smashed him against the ground again and again until he was hardly recognizable. He was hefted up over the Silencer's head with finality, and then the bloody pulp that had once been Doctor Alonzo Morris was thrown to the darkness below.

Shui arrived first and promptly skidded to a halt, staring down the construct which twisted its form to look at him. Xal was next, a sight slower but still miraculously on their feet. "What's the holdup – *woah*!" Xal peered around Shui and looked past the construct to look at Sunny. "Sunny?" they called nervously.

Sunny said nothing, staring down over the edge where Alonzo had been thrown. Her heart pounded in her chest, but her hands did not shake. It almost felt like a dream.

"Sunny?" Shui called, louder this time, and she blinked and looked up to find the Silencer still standing protectively between her and her companions.

"It's alright," she said. She pulled herself to her feet. "It's alright," she said, more softly this time, directly to the Silencer. "You know, don't you?"

The Silencer eyed her with its blank faceplate. It straightened up, towering over everyone by at least a head, and shifted into a different stance. Not a relaxed stance, but no longer quite such an aggressive one.

"Sunny, I hate to ask, but … " Xal had already forgotten the first construct, their gaze drawn to the monster in the center of the room. "You're not … you're not about to plug your dad into that, are you?"

Sunny looked back at the behemoth. "Yes," no longer seemed like the right answer. "I was going to," didn't ring quite true either.

"It's what he wanted," Sunny said, but even those words rang hollow in her ears.

"Sunny … " Shui winced. "I know I said we'd help, but this … " It was hard to explain the enormity of it, the canyon between the idea and the horrific reality.

"I know." Her voice trembled, and her hand shook. "I know," she said again, stronger this time. She shook her head. "I don't think I can do it." She held up the lattice, turning it this way and that. "It ain't him. We don't have the technology to pull ghosts

102

outta folks anymore, this is … it ain't him. He's already moved on to whatever's next, like we were supposed to."

The construct dipped its head, as though it were agreeing.

"And – and even if we did have the tech, and it was his ghost in here," Sunny barreled on, "it still wouldn't be him, not like how he was." The same way she wasn't who she'd been. "And even if it was perfect – " Her voice got real quiet. "This ain't living. It's just prolonged death."

Silence fell heavy in the room.

"Not for nothin'," Xal drawled after a bit, "but maybe we shouldn't be putting nothin' in that thing regardless." Followed by a soft "*oof*!" as Shui elbowed them in the ribs.

Sunny held the lattice heavy in her hand. It was small, had been small this entire time, but now it suddenly felt enormous. This was it, she realized with a sudden jolt of panic. This was the last piece she had of Dr. Quill.

All the bitterness in her, the anger over the enormity of his ask and his disregard for everything she was, warred with a sudden and profound emptiness yawning in her. She hadn't thought about it all. It was too soon, too fresh, and it hadn't mattered anyway because he said he'd be with her again.

Except, now, he never would.

The wound in her split apart, ragged and sore and bloody. She held the lattice to her chest. Would it be so bad to keep the copy? They'd never tested it; maybe it would be so like the original that she wouldn't notice. That she could pretend. It would be like he never died.

With a sudden start, the pit in her widened into a gulf. Those were probably the same thoughts running through her father's mind before he put her in the machine.

"Sunny ... " Shui started to approach, but stopped at the look the Silencer gave him.

"I know," Sunny whispered. She breathed, felt her chassis expand and contract, felt the false nerves relaying the information to her brain. Breathed again, one last time. Lifted her arm, and flung the crystal lattice into the depths to join Alonzo's body.

She didn't cry. She couldn't cry. She'd done enough crying.

Sunny wiped her cheeks anyway, even though there weren't any tears, and turned to the other construct. "Can you speak?" she asked.

The answer was a horrible garbled "Yes," and nothing more. Sunny nodded sympathetically.

"Were you awake during the Shattering? The, um, the big earthquake," Sunny elaborated. The construct paused, then shook its head. Whatever question Sunny had planned to ask flew out the window to make room for a more important one: "Do you want to see the surface?"

"Sunny, I don't think this is a good idea," Shui said quickly.

"Why not?" Sunny protested, though she already knew. "Why do I get to go around while they – " The construct held up a hand and shook its head. Sunny vibrated with the unfairness of it all before an idea came to her. "What if I added your lattice to my own?" she asked. "Then I – I could smuggle your ghost out next to mine. Find a medium, someone who can help us both move on."

Xal whistled low. "Is that really somethin' you can do?"

Sunny gave a wry smile. "I'm a scrapper. I'm good at this kind of thing." She looked back to the construct. "Would you – ?"

The construct folded in a perfect bow, and it emanated a single, garbled, "Please."

8

All in all, the process took what felt simultaneously like an eternity and a second, but in reality was close to an hour. Xal and Shui left the constructs to their work, occasionally looking up whenever Sunny said something particularly interesting or the magi-mechanical frequencies caught their ears. Mostly, they focused on the map.

"It'd be rough, but I might be able to climb out," Xal said, rolling a shoulder. "I feel a sight better than before."

"I couldn't," Shui said, sighing exhaustedly. The longer Sunny worked, the more his adrenaline had faded, and the more his bodily aches came to the forefront. He had his water on him, like any good wastelander, but water could only go so far. His ribs ached, and he felt as though he were more bruise than body. He chewed thoughtfully on a strip of jerky before offering Xal some. Xal took the offering with gusto. "Shame about the elevator, would've been nice to take it back up."

"The what?" No matter how long Shui squinted at Xal's expression, it never shifted from blank confusion.

" ... Nevermind," he said, deciding he was too tired to deal with it. "Don't worry about it."

"Can't wait to get back to Lacey," Xal said, taking Shui's words to heart.

"Lacey?"

"My raptor, sweetest li'l thing. Gorgeous white plumage, fastest ride in the Wastes," Xal bragged, puffing their chest out.

"Did y'all hide her? I don't think we saw her on the way in."

"Prob'ly." Xal folded their hands behind their head and leaned against the wall. "Don't 'xactly remember, but I wouldn't be without her if she weren't safe."

"What do you mean you don't remember?" Shui's attention had completely left the map by this point, fully focused on Xal.

Xal shrugged, then looked at him pointedly and tapped their forehead. "Ain't easy thinkin' with holes in your brain."

Shui's mouth hung open. "You're saying this entire time you had ... *no* idea what was going on?!" Xal grinned. "You seem *very* calm about this."

Xal shrugged. "Bigger things to worry about."

"And now?"

Xal shrugged again. "Don't seem to matter none now either."

"Is – is this normal? How do you live like this?"

"Being hard to kill probably helps."

Shui was saved from having to figure out how to respond by Sunny approaching. "All done," she said, causing the other two to sit up with their full attention.

"What's it like?" Xal asked.

"Strange." Sunny gave a lopsided grin. "I'm the only one with access to my body, but it's like he's riding side-saddle."

"He?" Shui asked.

"His name is Randal Watch." Sunny's eyes grew distant, and Shui and Xal watched as she flipped through memories that did not belong to her. "He was a soldier – well, emphasis on *was*, he was a military convict. They figured using someone who was already combat trained for something like this" – she gestured blankly back towards the empty killing machine behind her – "would make things easier." She paused, cocked her head to the side as though she were listening to something. "He says he knows a way out, but first he has a favor to ask."

"Another favor?" Shui asked.

Sunny ignored him. "He wants us to destroy this place, and I agree." She shook her head. "This place should be left in the past. We can't risk anyone like Alonzo finding it and attempting to pick up where the 'Fore-Folks left off."

"That would require a pretty big explosion," Xal pointed out. "'Fraid I left my dynamite in my other chaps."

"All of the chassis were built with a self-destruct sequence in case they ever fell into the wrong hands." Sunny didn't elaborate on who the "wrong hands" might belong to, nor that the

'Fore-Folks' hands maybe hadn't been entirely "right." "We set the big one to blow and call it a day."

"Alright, but how do we keep from getting caught in that?" Shui asked.

"Burrower tunnels," Sunny answered simply. "Watch has been keeping an eye on them, he says he knows where the tunnels are. We can take them to the surface."

Shui closed his eyes, mentally preparing himself for more effort.

"Shame about any of them getting caught in the blast," Xal lamented. "They're cute li'l rascals."

"If we blow up Watch's chassis first, it might startle them enough to get moving. They've mostly cleared out with all the commotion, anyway. We'll just have to take the risk."

"Well I, for one, cannot *wait* to get out of here," Xal said, getting to their feet. Shui followed suit, albeit more slowly and with more grumbling. Sunny waited, staring at him until he responded.

Shui sighed. "No time like the present."

Sunny's smile was exhausted and small and filled with the giddy joy of anticipated relief.

"Get ready to run," she said, then jogged back across the catwalk. She stopped at Watch's chassis, then climbed the metal stairs to lean precariously over to the monstrous construct. Then she was done and racing back towards them at a dead sprint. She said nothing, didn't hardly slow, just blew past them knowing they would follow.

Xal and Shui were hard-pressed to keep Sunny in sight, but they didn't dare ask her to slow down. She twisted through the halls without even needing to glance at the map, directed by a voice only she could hear. She skidded to a halt at the end of a hall that had been mostly destroyed, covered in rubble and debris, and at the end where the wall had been pulverized the most, a hole had been burrowed through.

"Up here," Sunny said, not bothering to gasp. "They head out to the surface." Without waiting for a response, she dove in. Xal followed without hesitation. Shui followed with as much hesitation as he dared, which wasn't very much at all. The tunnels were lightless, cramped and suffocating, barely large enough for Sunny to scramble through, much less Shui. Their heads scraped along the soil, their hands growing dirtier and dirtier as they dug their way through. All around them were the sounds of small, scurrying feet.

The first explosion was small, relatively speaking, just enough for sound and noise, but it did what it was supposed to. Between the intruders and the loud noise and the commotion that had been raging all day, the little colony of burrowers decided enough was enough and took to the proverbial hills. The skittering of little feet quickly became a torrent, buoying them and carrying them along with the tide.

"Faster – !" Sunny hissed. Neither Shui nor Xal had the breath to tell her they were moving as fast as they could.

They felt the rumbling before the roar of the explosion echoed its way through the tunnels. The squeaks and squawks of the burrowers grew louder and more panicked as the ground shook and danced and all three of them discovered that maybe they could, in fact, go faster. The second explosion shook the earth like the Shattering itself, causing a chain reaction in the ancient and fractured laboratory. Eons of suffering broke and exploded, and the heat hunted its way through the tunnels after them like a hungry predator. They scrambled as best as they could, even when their best seemed like it couldn't possibly be good enough to escape the hungry earth. They dug and dug and dug until –

Sunny gasped like a diver coming up for air as she breached the surface. Xal and Shui crawled out after her, hacking up dust and dirt as, around them, panicked burrowers fled into the night.

The trio fell to the ground as the aftershocks shuddered and shook and finally fell silent. For a moment no one spoke. The dust and sand beneath them was coarse and grainy; a cool wind nearly took Xal's hat with it, blowing off to some of the distant plateaus and mesas rising up from the earth; not too far away from the three of them was the entrance to the deep, deep canyon they'd all ventured into to start the whole mess;

above them stars littered the darkness, slowly dimming as the sky quietly began to lighten.

Xal broke the silence with a sudden, whooping laugh. "How's that for an exit?" they crowed, giddy with elation.

Despite herself, Sunny found herself giggling along. Shui focused on catching his breath but did crack a smile under his half-mask.

"Hey, Sunny?" he asked when his breathing had evened out.

"Yeah?" she said, still a little breathless herself.

"When you leave to find that medium, I could, y'know, go with," Shui offered. "Make sure no one gets your body when it's empty. If, y'know, you're interested."

Sunny was quiet with thought for a moment. "Honestly," she said, "I just want to make it to the next town over. We can figure things out there. And, well" – she rolled her head over to look at him – "if you wanted to come with, I can't rightly say I'd mind having someone extra to talk it over with." She looked back to the third member of their little trio. "Xal?"

Xal had sat up and was looking off to the distance, as though they were listening to a sound only they were privy to. Sunny couldn't hear a thing.

"Xal?" she tried again, and this time they looked back to her as though they'd forgotten there were other folks they were sitting in the Wastes with. "What about you? Are you gonna join us?"

Xal turned back to look off into the distance. "Not sure I can," they admitted.

"What about – just – just until the next town, then?" There was a sudden, familiar desperation building in her, the vertigo of sudden ends, the abrupt understanding that she would never see her strange friend again. But, then, Xal smiled back at her as dawn's rosy fingers began slipping over the horizon.

"Don't worry 'bout me, I'll be alright," they said. "But ... I reckon I could make it that far."

Across the dunes, a lone raptor crooned into the dawn. Xal's attention snapped to it, and they whooped as though the melancholy had already been forgotten. They put their hand to their mouth and whistled four sharp notes in response, and Lacey crooned the four notes right back as dawn fully broke.

—·—

Glossary

Burrower. The common name for *Oryctodromeus*! They were a small, fast-running dinosaur that dug tunnels and burrows. Despite being non-avian, they were still feathered like their raptor cousins!

Construct. An artificial creature created by the 'Fore-Folks out of metal and magic for various tasks.

Crystal Lattice. A device made of interlocking rings inlaid with crystals for the purpose of storing and releasing magic and spellwork. Size can range from small enough to fit in your hand, to ancient ones that encircled the planet. Most tech these days runs on them, though they are significantly less impressive than they were before the Shattering.

'Fore-Folks. The colloquial name for the civilization that existed before the Shattering – as well as the civilization that caused it. Any knowledge about them is merely speculation based on what they left behind.

Medium. Someone who speaks to and deals with ghosts.

Plasmashot. A type of gun that fires concentrated magic rather than bullets. It's very difficult to make; anyone seen with one in the modern era either scrapped it from some ruins, or they paid very handsomely for someone else to find or make one for them.

Raptor. A catch-all term for dinosaurs in the Dromaeosaur family! They aren't very useful for hauling, but they are quite popular for solo-riders and bandits. The most common breed of raptor is based off of the *Utahraptor* – the largest known Dromaeosaur! Lacey, meanwhile, is a *Dakotaraptor*, which are slightly smaller but faster and more agile.

Scrapper. The job title of those who undertake the lucrative and deadly job of taking things the 'Fore-Folks left behind and turning them into something useful.

Spellslinger. A person with the capacity and talent to bend magic to their will by whistling specific frequencies. Most tunes are taught and passed down from person to person, but that's not stopping folks from experimenting – leading to wondrous and disastrous results.

Spikeback. A catch-all term for Thyreophora dinosaurs, such as the *Stegosaurus* or the *Ankylosaurus*! They're popular with caravans for their natural protections and overall sturdiness.

The Shattering. An apocalyptic event brought on by the 'Fore-Folks that rendered most of their tech destroyed or inert and killed most of the population. There are no firsthand accounts of the event, so there is no way to know just what happened. Most folks have surmised, however, that whatever happened, it ended with planet-cracking earthquakes and pockets of magic erupting that were so concentrated and wild that hardly anything can live there anymore.

Tri-horn. A catch-all term for Chamosaurine dinosaurs, the most common being the *Triceratops*! They're generally used for hauling heavy loads.

The Wastes. Colloquial term for the stretch of battered, dusty, deadly wasteland that stretches from settlement to settlement.

Wilder-Folks. A catch-all term for intelligent, non-human creatures that live out in the Wastes and sometimes co-mingle with humans, often as tricksters or dealers.

About the Author

Kras Nebula is a little guy who's been writing things since they were even littler. They are a lover of everything sci-fi and fantasy. When not writing, they're probably playing with fiber, and have just recently gotten into drop-spinning their own yarn! Wow!

— • —

BEFORE YOU GO

This is the sixth book in 12 Months of Whump, a series of whumpy novellas published by WPP throughout 2025. Each novella can be read as a standalone.

To stay up to date with the 12 Months of Whump series and other whumperfly-inducing projects, visit us at https://thewhumpyprintingpress.tumblr.com/

.